# VERONICA

Derek Symes, newly arrived to take up a job in Cape Town, is strongly attracted to Veronica Arendse, a lovely coloured girl, the daughter of a teacher-writer father and an actress mother.

Derek is transferred and believes the affair with Veronica to be at an end. On his return to Cape Town he falls irrevocably in love with Lindy van Vuuren, an open-minded university student, the daughter of an old Cape family.

It is after his marriage to Lindy that Derek realizes that his thoughtless liaison with Veronica has landed both him and Lindy in a position bristling with danger, responsibility and the makings of tragedy.

# VERONICA

A NOVEL BY
Joy Packer

EYRE & SPOTTISWOODE · LONDON

*First published 1970*
*Reprinted twice 1970*
*Copyright © 1970 Joy Packer*
*Printed in Great Britain for*
*Eyre & Spottiswoode (Publishers) Ltd*
*11 New Fetter Lane, E.C.4*
*by Cox & Wyman Ltd,*
*Fakenham, Norfolk*

SBN 413 44600 X

1.3

3.74p

AUTHOR'S NOTE

All the characters in this novel are entirely
fictitious.

Joy Packer, Cape Peninsula

# CONTENTS

# CONTENTS

# I

# LINDY

---

*'That sewing-girl, Veronica Arendse'*

The moment Veronica entered the house I was aware of the inevitable chip on her shoulder. It was reflected in her manner, which was both haughty and polite, and in the slightly resentful expression of her oblique almond eyes as she cast a quick interested glance round our large living-room. A tiny muscle twitched above her left cheekbone and I had a momentary impression that she was seeing ghosts.

'You've made this place very nice, Mrs Symes,' she said. 'I could never have believed it was the same house.' Her voice was soft and husky. Educated.

'You knew it before?' I asked.

'Oh, yes, well.'

She shrugged out of her neat threadbare winter coat and slipped her gloves into the pocket. She stood, holding it over her arm, rather tall for one of her race, very slim with high aggressive breasts thrusting against her cherry-red polo-necked sweater and protuberant buttocks straining at her short, tight skirt. Her legs

9

were slender and her feet and hands very small. She had
'oosened the gaily patterned scarf round her head and
her heavy black hair hung, straight and glossy, to her
shoulders. She was light skinned, only her soft full lips
and small flattened nose betrayed her mixed ancestry.
She tossed her head in a gesture embracing the fire
blazing in the hearth, the archway giving a glimpse of
the dining-room beyond and the sliding doors opening
on to a covered stoep and a walled patio shaded by
cypresses and the great oaks of the Cape Peninsula. It
was damp and autumnal now, but in summer, when the
roses and honeysuckle are in bloom, it is the secluded
centre of our existence.

'I remember this house when it was still two cottages,'
she said. 'My auntie lived here and my cousin was next
door – there on the other side of that door.'

She spoke without rancour but with lively curiosity
in her voice and suddenly it flashed into my mind that
that was why she had been willing to come to me. A
good sewing-woman is a treasure my friends are
seldom ready to share and it hadn't been easy to per-
suade old Ann Seymour from next door to ask Veronica
Arendse to spare me two days. Veronica was one of
Ann's discoveries. Ann has a gift for nosing out
coloured 'treasures' – carpenters, electricians, plumbers
and people like 'my sweet char' or 'my dear gardener –
a bit simple but so *tender* with the plants'. She lives
alone and she has time to talk to them a lot. That way

one tells her of another and they all like her. But only if you are one of her privileged special friends will she pass them on.

'Veronica's booked to the eyebrows,' Ann had said. 'I'm sure there isn't a hope.'

'You could try her.'

'Well, I'll mention it but don't tell a soul. If everybody's after her she'll put up her prices. She's done that once already. She's rather a curious girl. Independent – almost bolshie – but well-mannered. A coloured *lady*, my dear.'

Ann rang me up a few days later to say, 'Veronica Arendse seems anxious to go to you. She's going to fit you in. It's odd because she told me some time ago she couldn't cope with any new engagements.'

So here Veronica was. There was a sound like a bombardment on the corrugated iron roof of the stoep and her face broke into a smile that made it surprisingly attractive and somehow fairer. She had good teeth – rare among the coloureds.

'Acorns,' she said. 'I remember! At this season they drop from the big oak on to the roof.'

'That's right. It's the theme song of autumn. If you like, I'll show you over the house. The main bedroom's here adjoining this room – where your cousin's cottage used to be.'

I led her into the pretty suite comprising our bedroom and bathroom and Derek's dressing-room and then back past the cosy warmth of the living-room fire into the short entrance passage with doors into Derek's study and my sewing-room on one side and a spare double bedroom and bath on the other. The kitchen and pantry backing the dining-room were airy and spacious with the yard, maid's room, shower, toolshed and car-port beyond. The conversion had been cleverly accomplished when the area, which had till fairly recently been coloured, was proclaimed white. Scores of cottages formerly occupied by coloured people had been rebuilt to create the fashionable Chelsea-type homes that were fetching high prices in the southern suburbs of Cape Town. It was all part of the Government plan for segregated living.

'I could never have believed it,' said Veronica Arendse. 'You live here with your husband – and family—'

'We have no family.' It was a sore point.

'Well, there's room and there's time.' She assessed me frankly. We were probably of an age. I was twenty-four and Derek and I had been married three years.

'When my auntie and my cousin occupied these cottages there were – let me see' – she counted on her fingers, her soft full lips silently enunciating names – 'nineteen people living here. Three generations crowded into poky rooms, sharing beds, no place for the children to do their homework in peace, hardly space for my auntie to set up her machine – she was a sewing-

12

woman like I am – or to turn in the kitchen. Your stoep was a sleep-out for the boys.'

'Where is she now? Your auntie.'

She made a contemptuous gesture. 'In a council house miles away on the Flats. The house is all right, but it's far from her husband's work, and the boys' too, and her neighbours are not the type she'd choose – bad company for the girls. Here she had respectable people living around her. It's the same for my cousin. When people are turned out of an area they have to go where they can get accommodation. After generations in a neighbourhood with school, church and work near by, it's upsetting to be thrown out and told to start again.'

Her sense of injustice smouldered under the softly spoken reproach. We were in my sewing-room and a spatter of rain beat against the window-pane. My sewing-machine stood on the big worktable and the dresses to be altered were hanging in the built-in cupboard. I opened it and explained what I wanted done.

'These I must try on,' I said. 'I have pins and reels of different coloured cottons and silk but if there's anything you need I can get it when I go out to do my shopping.'

She nodded, and I watched her quick deft fingers pinning seams or gussets as I stood in front of the long mirror on the inside of the open cupboard door. She knelt to raise a hem, using the rule measure she had brought with her. I thought, there but for the grace of God, kneel I. My own face looked back at me, fair skinned, faintly freckled, butter-coloured hair cut short to accentuate the boyish shape of my head and the length of my neck and rather sloping shoulders. The natural make-up trend suited me with my short blunt nose and curly mouth. My eyes, smoky blue and wide set under well-marked brows, looked back at me with a puzzled expression.

Like Ann, it amused me to talk to people, to find out what made them tick, and Veronica interested me. But she troubled me too. Even the brief contact of having her touch my body as she fitted me was disturbing in a strange unaccountable way, as if her hands were transmitting some message I was reluctant to receive. I remembered Ann Seymour's words 'Veronica seems anxious to go to you —' Why? Was it just interest in the telescoped cottages that had once been inhabited by her relatives? Or was it something else – something more intimate? I looked down at her bowed head with the blue sheen of a starling's wing in the hair that fell across her cheek. It was a proud head. She was one of the few who didn't simply accept the fate allotted to her. She was a rebel. Where would it get her?

She rose and helped me step out of the dress.

'It's three years old,' I said. 'But the material is good. It was part of my trousseau.'

14

'Your things are worth altering. Expensive clothes usually are.'

'I'm going to the shopping-centre now. Is there anything you need?'

'I don't think so.'

'Minnie'll bring you coffee and biscuits at eleven. Or would you rather have tea?'

'Coffee, please.'

When I went into the lane she was bent over the machine and Minnie was banging about in the kitchen, smashing something, no doubt. They were poles apart, Minnie and Veronica, and yet people always lump the coloureds together in their minds. They can't seem to recognize that there are as many grades among that community as there are among our own. I thought of Veronica with her natural elegance and soft voice and found myself flushing that she should have to eat her lunch in the kitchen with Minnie. She'd have been more suitable company for me.

But, in fact, when one o'clock came and she knocked off work for an hour, I heard her laughing in the kitchen with Minnie and chattering in Afrikaans. She was clearly adaptable. A bit of an actress perhaps, a born mimic. They all were. Variable, moody, a sad-happy, singing, dancing, irresponsible people existing for the day in a caul of apathy. 'Why should we try? Where does it get us?' Yet there are many who fight for their children with fierce spurts of energy – to give them an education that will fit them for a better future and work that is not in some white woman's house or her husband's fields and vineyards. They dream a little for their ever-increasing families.

In the afternoon, when Veronica was fitting me for the gay psychodelic blouse she was making to go with my new shocking-pink slacks, I said:

'Do you want me to pay you for today? Or would you rather I settled with you for both days tomorrow?'

'Tomorrow will do.'

'And there's your bus fare. Do you have far to go?'

'District Six. My father has a nice little house there – high up with a view of the Bay. The Government will take it from us and move us out to the Flats. The school too. My father is Principal of the secondary school across the road from us as my grandfather was before him.'

The coloured area on the slopes of Table Mountain on Cape Town's southern limit was to be cleared and rebuilt for whites. Many of us were furious about the removal of the coloureds but our protests were as much use as whispers on the wind.

'It's fresh where we live,' she went on, 'though a lot of District Six is hot and windy. My God, how the south-easter comes over the mountain there! It's enough to blow the children off the face of the earth. Of course most of the place is a slum, but not our bit.'

Her voice was truculent as if she'd be pleased to see the future tenants of the newly proclaimed white area whipped out to sea by the summer gales.

I took off the blouse and folded it and put it with the other garments waiting to be completed next day.

'Are you married, Veronica?' Families often shared the same house and the grandmother minded the children while the young couple were at work.

'No, Mrs Symes. I live with my father. My mother is dead and my sisters are in Kimberley.'

'You should have a husband. Too choosy, I suppose.'

'Yes.' She smiled.

I wanted to ask if she had children. Among her people the illegitimate child is the rule rather than the exception. Certainly it's no disgrace – nor is it anywhere, these days, for that matter – but something in her expression, in the set of her lips and shoulders, warned me that the subject was closed. She was not unfriendly but she had a certain dignity. She could, with a glance or a gesture, retreat and become aloof.

'If I can have a dustpan and a broom I can clear up this mess of threads and pins on the carpet,' she offered.

'That's all right. Minnie'll do it tomorrow before you come.'

She glanced at her watch. It was after five o'clock. 'Then I'll be off.'

She slipped on her coat and tied the scarf loosely over her hair. She put gloves on her small hands. The rain had stopped and the air outside smelled of leaf-mould and bonfires – smoky, damp April air with winter on the threshold.

'It'll be spring in England,' she said unexpectedly.

'Yes. A lovely month of blossom and flowering shrubs.'

'Minnie told me you were going to England soon. That'll be nice.'

'It's a business trip for my husband, a holiday for me. We'll only be away a few weeks. My husband looks forward to seeing old friends again. He's English.'

'So Minnie said. It'll be a treat for you both. Good-bye, Mrs Symes.'

'Good-bye, Veronica. See you tomorrow.'

She walked briskly down the lane towards the Main Road and I went back to the patio where I had been pruning the first of our rose bushes. The oak leaves lay thick on the ground, acorns plopped noisily on to the roof with every gust of wind and the violet shoulder of Devil's Peak rose against the apricot evening sky. Soon, when the branches were bare, more of the mountain would be visible. I loved our pretty home yet this evening I had a curious feeling about it. Only a few years ago this roof – leaking like a sieve then – had sheltered nineteen people, the dispossessed now exiled to abodes on the windy desolate Flats. I was uneasy. I found myself almost wishing that Veronica Arendse had refused to sew for me.

It was dusk when Derek came home. I heard the double blast on the horn that was his signal as he turned into the car-port and immediately my sombre mood lightened. A few minutes later I heard his step as he crossed the red-tiled stoep on to the patio. His step? A buoyant stride, characteristic of my tall lean exuberant man. I turned to see his wide happy smile even more sparkling than usual. A little gold filling glinted in an upper tooth, the wind tossed his hair back from his broad forehead. Chestnut hair, the colour of a thoroughbred horse's coat, hazel eyes with little gold speckles in their laughing depths. He put his arms round me and gave me a hug and a kiss. He always kissed me as if he meant it and his homecoming was something that was with me all day – a looking forward.

'I've got some exciting news.' His voice was warm like his smile, mellow and English. People were always pleased to hear it, to have him around made them feel good, as if the world were a brighter place. He knew that and sometimes he traded on it but more often he was genuinely glad of his own heart-lifting quality. 'A wonderful personality – so optimistic,' our friends said, and smiled tolerantly at a certain weakness that was the fault of his virtues, a tendency to gamble, engendered by his firm belief that everything would come right and a disregard for the morrow, as if all his great vitality must be expended today lest tomorrow never come. His effect on others was invigorating, if transitory, leaving a sort of afterglow. He made women feel more feminine, men more successful, children more important and the old younger. I was still as susceptible as anyone else to his charm even if three years of marriage had taught me to beware of a certain instability, even secrecy. At times, in repose, when he was unconscious of being watched, his engaging irregular features were steeped in a curious sadness that troubled me. He was quite unaware of it and at the first word from me his face would change and clear – but I had seen the cloud and wondered about it.

'Exciting news? Tell me, quick!'

'We're not just going to Europe for a business and holiday jaunt. We're to be posted to London for two years so I can make my number with the London directors and get the hang of that end of the business. After that I'll probably be appointed Managing Director here in Cape Town.'

I laughed, excited too, but discounting the final conclusion.

'Managing Director here? You'll only be twenty-eight in two years' time!'

'The accent is on youth today.'

'The present Managing Director is fifty.'

'They'll take him back to the London office, I expect. Give him a final run for his money before retiring him.'

'You expect? You mean you hope!'

'I'll mix a martini,' he laughed. 'This is a celebration.'

I pulled off my gardening gloves and went to wash my hands. When I came back into the living-room he had taken bottles and glasses out of the corner cupboard and I heard him calling to Minnie on the other side of the dining-room hatch. 'Ice, Minnie, and a lemon and a sharp knife,' and there was the usual slamming of the fridge door and clatter of cubes into the plastic ice-bowl as Minnie obliged in her rough and ready fashion.

'This is a silly time for a martini,' I said. 'We should have it just before dinner, not now when I haven't had time to change out of my gardening slacks.'

He was singing to himself as he measured out lavish gin and negligible vermouth and sliced a thin strip of lemon peel. He added the ice and when he had stirred the clear pale cocktail, he filled two glasses and handed me one.

'To London – and us!'

'To London – and us,' I echoed.

I flopped into a deep easy chair near the fire.

'When do we go?'

'In two months' time. By sea.'

'But we'll have to arrange to let this house.'

'That'll be no trouble. People are screaming for houses. Specially these. They're fashionable. We'll get a fat rent.'

I knew it was true, not just his optimism.

'This house is a sensible size,' he added. 'There's plenty of accommodation for children if the tenants convert your little sewing-room into a bedroom.'

'Do we want tenants with children?'

'Perhaps not. Perhaps a couple would be better. We want it as good as new when we come home to it again.'

'I had a sewing-girl here today,' I said. 'Her relatives lived in these two cottages before they were converted. She said nineteen people slept under this roof.'

'Gross overcrowding, poor devils.'

'Four would be nice. You and me – and two children.'

The shadow crossed his face. For the past two years we had wanted to start a family. Nothing had happened. I'd been to a doctor who'd said I was perfectly normal. Too tense, perhaps. I must relax and stop worrying. My longing for a child probably created tension in my husband. I had badgered Derek to go to a doctor too, but he'd refused. Now I returned to the attack.

'Maybe in London you wouldn't mind going to a specialist —'

'Please,' he said. 'Leave that subject alone. Just let nature take its course. It'll all happen as we hope one of these days.'

22

'That's what you always say. It's what you always believe – everything will go your way. If not now, then eventually. Sometimes one has to act.'

He put his glass on the mantelpiece where he had been standing with his back to the fire. He came to the chair in which I lounged and touched my hair with gentle exploratory fingers.

'Darling, try not to fuss. Perhaps it's just as well there aren't any babies to take to London. Let's live for the next move. It's going to be interesting and fun and I get a good rise in salary and various perks.'

So we began to plan the immediate future and I caught fire from his enthusiasm. There was going to be a lot to do in the next few weeks.

'That sewing-girl,' I said, 'Veronica Arendse – I'll have to book her again next month. She's very difficult to get and I'll need —'

Derek had been about to take up his glass when he – who was so seldom clumsy – knocked it off the mantelpiece. It shattered on the hearth.

'Our Stuart Crystal!' I cried. 'Oh, Derek!'

He was stooping to pick up the fragments and throw them into the fire. He must have been careless again for he lifted his hand and sucked his forefinger.

'You've cut it?'

'It's nothing.' He straightened up. 'A little blood-letting is a good thing.'

23

But I saw that it was bleeding profusely and he was pale as if he felt suddenly sick.

'Come on,' I said. 'We'll bind it up with Elastoplast.'

Somehow the small accident took the joy and exhilaration out of the evening.

# 2

## DEREK

---

*'She set me on fire'*

When Lindy said 'That sewing-girl – Veronica Arendse,' my heart turned turtle and went plummeting down into the pit of my stomach.

Veronica in this house! She must have known it was mine. Why had she come? She didn't need the work. I never for a moment doubted some important ulterior motive. And I'd been so careful. She was paid every month by my friend and lawyer, John Burford. John is a good fellow, he'd understood the whole wretched situation and had taken care of it. We'd made sure that she and I should never meet. And here she'd been, right in my home, sewing for my wife, preparing to come again. And Lindy so perceptive, so sensitive!

My parents are dead but my father was English and my mother American, a New Yorker, and I have none of the built-in race prejudice of South Africans. In that way it hasn't been easy for me to settle down here. Too many aspects of the political set-up infuriate me. I try to close my eyes to it and enjoy the advantages which are many. It's in my nature to evade what upsets me. But in the circumstances it's difficult. My conscience is doubly vulnerable. White decrees decide where brown people shall live, what work they shall do, where their children shall play, what beaches they may bathe from, what transport they may use, what cinemas they may attend, what schools and hospital wards can receive them. Yet between person and person there's immense good will. Lindy and her friends are for ever collecting for coloured or African welfare, and, when she talks with folk like Minnie or our coloured occasional gardener, she does so with genuine friendliness and a special quick humour that leaps between the inhabitants of the Cape, white or brown.

Lindy knows the coloured people with her blood and her bones. Her mother's ancestors came to the Cape with the first Dutch settlers in the seventeenth century and her father's forebears not much later. Those early Dutch landowners were good to their slaves on the whole, and, in the nineteenth century it was the custom to christen and free the children of slaves long before my mother's people were fighting the southerners in the American Civil War. The Cape coloureds are the progeny of imported African and Malay slaves, mixed with infusions of white and Hottentot blood. In fact, every race which has ever contributed to South African history has left its mark on the coloured South Africans.

You'll see them waiting outside the Non-European Out Patients Department of any big hospital at the Cape – some dark as soot, others light haired and pale skinned who seem to have got into the wrong group. Girls like Veronica.

I met her when first I came to the Cape nearly five years ago. I'd been briefed by the firm. There was no excuse for what happened. Or was there? I believe perhaps there was, but then it is my habit to make excuses for myself – even *to* myself.

I was twenty-one then, not very old or wise, and the firm had taken a service bachelor flat for me in a barracks of a place at Three Anchor Bay. It was west-facing with a splendid view of the sea and on misty nights the fog-horn blared incessantly like a cow in labour – not that I've heard a cow in labour. When I say service, it didn't include meals but there were plenty of eating places round about and the flat had a kitchenette. I could knock up a meal for myself as well as the next person. I sent my soiled clothes to the laundry attached to the flats. That was really how it began.

Now I want to make one thing clear. I wasn't lonely. The staff of my firm – Aston Brothers Export and Import – introduced me to their families and friends and I met attractive unattached girls. The Cape girls are quite something – strong, healthy, pretty enough to eat, outdoor, indoor, the lot. Their morals are no different from anyone else's. If they fancy a boy that's that. The thing was I didn't want to get involved and find myself going steady. It can happen so fast. You sleep with a girl, and, let's face it, there is an obligation. I didn't want obligations. I wanted time to look around. I used to wake up in the mornings and see that great stretch of surf and sea and sky with the sun-glitter on the water and I'd take huge gulps of fresh bright air and think, Here I am in this gorgeous country – sea, mountains, forests, friendly people and a good job – and I'm free, free as this strong salty air!

I'd been in the flat about a fortnight when she tapped on the door and came in. I'd just got back from town. It was about six on a spring evening.

'Mr Symes,' she said. 'I've come to explain about your laundry. One of the girls was careless ironing your pyjama jacket, she burnt a hole in the back. I've patched it as best I could.'

She held out the pyjama jacket and showed me the neat patch. Even I could see she'd made an expert job of it – the stripes just right. I could also see that she was very pretty and she had a soft attractive voice.

'I stole from inside the hem,' she explained.

'You'd never be able to tell,' I said. 'You can certainly sew.'

'I work here in the flats. I'm in charge of the linen, sorting, mending, all that. But our laundry isn't too good when it comes to personal things. Would you like me to do your shirts and pyjamas and so on? I could find the time.'

'Why, yes, I'd be delighted.'

We made a satisfactory arrangement. She put the laundry on my bed and pointed to the pyjama jacket.

'Do you want to make a fuss about this? Tell the management and so on? It would get the girl into trouble.'

'I'd hate to get any girl into trouble.' I grinned and she smiled back, her slant eyes dancing.

She was standing there in my bedsitter as if she was in no hurry to go and I wanted to ask her to sit down and have a drink with me, but I wasn't fool enough for that. Not then. I knew she wasn't white although her skin wasn't really dark – light olive, I'd say – and her black hair was straight and shiny, coiled into the nape of her long slender neck. Her features were small and prettily moulded with the softness of putty. She wore a starched white overall with a belt and her waist was tiny. She was very slim and I was thinking how good she'd look in a bikini and how small her hands were and how brilliant her eyes.

'What's your name?' I asked.

'Veronica. Veronica Arendse.' She pronounced the e at the end of her surname as if it were an a.

'When will you come for my odds and ends, Miss Arendse?'

She laughed. 'You needn't be quite so formal, Mr

Symes. I'm just Veronica here. I have a key to the flats. Leave your stuff in the linen basket in the bathroom and I'll collect it tomorrow morning and I'll bring it back on Friday. You can pay me by the month.'

'Thank you,' I said. 'That'll be fine.'

She went out, trim and fresh, and I heard her quick step along the corridor and then I couldn't hear it any more. When I went to the fridge to get myself a beer, her eyes laughed at me under the foam, the colour of beer but more intoxicating. It couldn't go on like this, I thought. I must get myself a girl.

She collected and returned my laundry and mending while I was at work, so I didn't see her again until she came at the end of the month for her payment. This time she wasn't in her hygienic white overall. She wore tight slacks that spanned over her rather pronounced behind and a cotton T-shirt that proved I was right about thinking she'd be good in a bikini. I noticed that her nails were painted with iridescent varnish the colour of ginger.

'You have beautiful hands,' I said, and she flushed, her olive skin suddenly warm and glowing. But she ignored the compliment.

She took the notes from me and put them into her bag. There was a bright scarf around her throat and I longed to touch her neck above it – to take it between my hands and make believe I'd strangle her, but so softly. Her hair wasn't pinned up this time, it flowed over her shoulders. I pulled a packet of cigarettes from my pocket.

'You smoke?'

She took one. 'Sometimes.'

I lit it for her and her lashes rested thick on her high cheekbones. Her eyebrows flared up at the outer corners like her bright eyes.

'Sit down,' I said. 'I'll get us a beer.'

'It wouldn't do if we were found talking like ordinary human beings,' she said with a funny bitter smile I got to know very well.

'I'll lock the door. I'm not in if anyone comes.'

When I came back with the beer she was sitting in the armchair near the divan. The chair was navy blue and her slacks were cherry red and her shirt was pale blue. Her sandals were red and her toenails were painted that iridescent ginger. Her feet, like her hands, were small.

'You're very new in this country,' she remarked. Her soft voice was a little husky, but I guessed she could yell all right in the company that called for yelling.

'Yes, I'm a new boy all right. Tell me a bit about South Africa.'

'Never do what you're doing now,' she said. 'Treat brown people like lepers or servants. Now tell me about England. What's it like where you come from?'

'I'm a Londoner. It's a great sprawling crowded city on a river. A river with boats and barges and seagulls

and down at the docks the ships come from far away
with all the cargoes of the wide world, and like as not
the dockers refuse to unload them because there's a
strike on.'

'Are there many coloured people in London?'

'Masses. All sorts. All they need is to belong to the
Commonwealth and they can come and live in the
Welfare State.'

'South Africa isn't in the Commonwealth. It's a
Republic. Even London wouldn't want our coloured
people any more. When they had British passports my
father says it was different.'

'What does your father do?'

'He's a teacher. He's Principal of a secondary school
in District Six. That's the coloured quarter on the other
side of Cape Town. He's a writer too. He writes
stories about District Six and the people who live
there. They're published in the papers. One day, when
he retires, he'll become a full-time writer. God knows
where we'll be living then – somewhere on the Flats.
Our area is zoned for white.'

'I know. It's all wrong. It should be rebuilt for your
own people. Tell me about your mother.'

'She died of TB last year. She was a singer – one of
the leads in the Eoan Group. That's our cultural group.
Opera, ballet, oratorios —'

She broke off at the sound of footsteps approaching
the flat. Someone knocked on my door. She put one

hand over her mouth and stubbed out her cigarette with the other. She looked terrified and turned her head as if she were seeking a hiding-place. Whoever it was went away and she rose hastily.

I caught her arms.

'Surely what I do in my own flat is my own business.'

'This isn't London,' she whispered with repressed fury. 'If you entertain a coloured girl in your flat you'll have to explain the reason why to the police! Do you realize that if you kissed me you could go to prison for it. Three months or more, and no option of a fine.'

It's true. You don't even have to be caught in the act, it's enough just to show the inclination. Where in the world except South Africa would you find such a cruel, ridiculous law as the Immorality Act which makes desire across the colour line a criminal offence! So I wanted her and she wanted me and it wasn't a question of money, though that came into it later.

It wasn't long before we began taking risks.

The night porter was a hunchback dwarf – a queer ugly little fellow who muttered to himself and walked with high soft steps like a cat on wet tiles. You could almost picture him shaking his feet like fastidious paws. He too lived in District Six with his wife and five children. He was some sort of family connection of Veronica's and she said he was safe. 'He won't give me away. He'd never want to hurt me.' I believed her. If he saw her leave her room at night and slip into my flat he certainly kept quiet about it. He had some sixth sense – or a good informer – for he never failed to warn her when the police were likely to raid the servants' quarter as they did periodically in search of Africans without passes or people hiding and purveying dagga – marijuana – or creating disturbances. I tipped him often and handsomely and he took the money, deadpan, with a grunt rather than a thank you. Nothing was ever said between us but I treated him as a look-out. I imagined that his feeling for Veronica was one of faithful if inarticulate devotion. She was the sort of girl who might easily make enemies among her own people. High hat. Danie Jacobs, the hunchback night watchman, was a valuable ally.

'His eldest son is at my father's school,' she told me once. 'He has clever children. Straight bodies too. Funny, isn't it? Danie's no fool. He has a finger in lots of pies in District Six. He makes betting books. He does well out of that.'

We were living dangerously, disobeying the social taboos of the country and deliberately violating one of its many laws.

'We're mad,' she said one night. 'One word of this and we'll both be in gaol. You'd be ruined.

'Get yourself a white girl,' she went on. 'It isn't as if you loved me.'

Suddenly her eyes were full of tears. I saw them brimming in the moonlight that flooded the room.

They hung on her lashes like crystal and detached themselves to roll down her cheeks and spill on to the white pillow-case. 'It's hard on me too,' she went on in a choked way. 'You make love to me as if you cared. Can you think what that means to a girl like me?'

'I care.'

It was true up to a point. I have always cared about the women I've slept with – wanted them to get as much out of it as I did myself. At least, almost always. But caring and loving are different. I certainly didn't love Veronica. She set me on fire and supplied a vital need which left me relaxed and at ease to dance and flirt with other girls and which had absolutely nothing to do with my steadily increasing social sphere. Love didn't enter my life till I met Lindy and by then it was all over with Veronica.

Aston Brothers decided to send me to Johannesburg for six months. I wish now that they had taken the decision a few weeks earlier!

It was the furtiveness I hated with Veronica yet in a way the knowledge that our association was a razor's edge added to its fascination. Anyone could have tipped off the police, any night there might have been a hammering on the door, discovery and disgrace. Jacobs, the dwarf, had only to say a word or make a gesture to land us both in the cart. We knew it but we became engulfed in a sort of euphoria. I was twenty-one, she was nineteen. There were hours when we just talked in the hot summer nights, whispering till the three o'clock sea breeze rose and cooled the air as the stars began to fade.

I learned a good deal about her childhood in the small solidly built house on the flank of Devil's Peak with the pine forests behind it and Table Bay below.

'The lights of the city and the bay and of the roads running north across the Flats and all the new towns – God, when I was a child I thought it was Fairyland down there! Ours is a respectable street where people try to better themselves – people like my pa. There are even a few white families up that way and Malays who live around the Mosque and some very nice Indians like Dr Pather. He's a good man and a friend of my father's. We all rely on Dr Pather. Lower down are shops and laundries and restaurants – mostly Indian and Malay – and it's quite gay. But in the side streets anything can happen. That's where the skollies and skelms hang about —'

'Skollies and skelms?'

'You'd call them thugs and rascals, I suppose. The boys who smoke reefers and drink dreadful liquor, boys who are runners for the gambling games and horses. A lot of them carry bicycle chains and knives, they steal and start fights and think nothing of killing people. And the noise on week-ends! On hot nights like this, when it's quiet here with just the sea, District

Six is loud with pop music, every window open because of the heat, every wireless with an amplifier, electric guitars, bands in places where you can dance, and above it all the wailing of ambulance sirens and the blue lights of police vans. We live round the bend from a slum and we can never forget it.'

She shivered and drew closer to me. This was her life, the borderline between safety and danger, between respectability and the dregs. She had a room in the servants' quarters of the flats. But there too the nights would often be made hideous by the violent private lives of the dark occupants. She had a shuddering hatred of the squalor and crime that surrounded her people like a red nimbus. She longed for security as a way of life, but she feared and despised the white authority that was paternal and benevolent, cruel and indifferent by turns.

'If you're coloured you must always be shutting your eyes,' she said. 'Trying not to see the dirt and the shabby bare-foot children waiting their turn to get into the schools that are overcrowded already, and all the many bad things that go on right under your nose day and night.'

'You'll be safer when I go to Johannesburg,' I said.

Then she'd begin to cry. But it was true.

'Does your father know about us?' I asked her once. She took fright immediately. 'Nobody knows. Not even a child must guess. A child might talk. My father would be afraid. He'd condemn me.'

'What about Jacobs, the hunchback?'

'He's all right. He talks to himself more than to other people.'

She imitated his mutterings and his high-stepping cat-in-the-rain prance so that the tall pretty girl became a deformed eccentric dwarf. We had to laugh after that.

I always hated it when she left me to go back to her room, a creature of the night flitting batlike through the cobweb grey of the small hours, unattended, taking her chances. But that was how it had to be even on our last night together before I went to Johannesburg. When I let her go just before daybreak my bare shoulder and my chest were wet with her tears. I'd given her some money and I never expected to see her again. I thought, when I came back I'd find another flat somewhere else. This had to be the end. We'd taken too many chances already. I'd been in South Africa long enough by then to realize the utter folly of what we'd been doing.

Johannesburg was exciting. What a city up there in the clear bright air of the high veld! What people! They know how to live – feverishly, making and losing fortunes, speculating on the Stock Exchange, smiling a little patronizingly, a little wistfully upon the conservative Cape.

The new tempo suited my mood. I had become too deeply enmeshed in my reckless double life in the Peninsula. Here I could escape it entirely for the next six months and by the time I was ready to resume my work in the Cape Town branch of Aston Brothers I would be able to make a new beginning. I saw few coloured people in Johannesburg. It is the city of contrasts, of rich well-fed whites and hungry Africans, of the gold mines and the compounds where the tribesmen come from their territories as indented labour to lead a restricted city life and as often as not to indulge in faction fights among themselves. It is a prosperous city of skyscrapers and mansions with beautiful gardens, of seething black townships and of magnificent hospitals and organized welfare for the black population. It is the hotbed of communist agitators where intrigue flourishes on discontent.

I was still unwilling to get entangled with a marriagable girl but I soon found myself attracted by a young grass-widow. Her husband was a scientist who had sailed for the South African Research Station in the Polar ice of Antarctica. He would be away for a year and Doris was not a girl to be left alone. If he used his imagination at all the poor devil must have suffered agonies. Doris was at a loose end, so was I. We enjoyed ourselves. We played tennis, we rode out across the veld, I acquired a small but fast car and we spent a long week-end in the Kruger Park Game

Sanctuary where I got my first impression of wild animals free in their own surroundings. Lion, elephant, leopards, every conceivable buck and all about us the dry aromatic peace of the thorn-veld and birds with jewelled plumage. When the time came I was reluctant to leave the Transvaal and return to the Cape. My six months up country had been a sort of emancipation.

Back in the Peninsula I took a small flat among the forests and oak avenues of Newlands not far from where we live now. If I went to the sea it was to the mild Indian Ocean waves of Muizenberg and Strandfontein, no longer to the cold crashing Atlantic combers of the Peninsula's west coast. I wanted everything to be different. I wanted to be shot of the guilt and fear that had haunted me during my association with Veronica. I became more available to the young set which quickly absorbed me. There were no more evasions, no more hurrying home from parties or dances because Veronica might be waiting to slip into my flat. Veronica was out of my life.

I grew very friendly with John Burford, a young solicitor who worked for our firm among other assignments. John was amusing and he was also remarkably astute, even brilliant in his job, and Aston Brothers put most of their legal problems into his hands. He is a specialist in Company Law and tax evasion and, one way and another, he has saved Aston Brothers a mint of money. He is two or three years older than I am. It was through him that I found my flat and joined a tennis club and was selected to play in League matches. John is a good player himself, one of those small vigorous performers who make up for lack of height and reach with speed, energy and footwork. He is tireless, with a humorous, pugnacious face and keen brown eyes. Women dote on him. It was through John and the Tennis Club that I met Lindy.

We'd just finished playing a single and were strolling over to the clubhouse when I saw her standing in the speckled shade of an oak watching a mixed double on court one. She wore a very short dress with a pleated skirt and a close fitting top and her long bare limbs were slim and evenly tanned. She carried her small honey-coloured head as if she owned the world. Her hair was cut short, and it gleamed like a golden cap. When she turned as we passed and smiled at John I felt as if I'd been hit over the heart. I stopped in my tracks and John glanced at me and stopped too.

'Hullo, Lindy,' he said. 'This is Derek Symes, a new member of our club. Derek, meet Belinda van Vuuren. She plays in our first team.'

I don't remember what I said or what I did. I only know that from then on Lindy was the one for me. The Committee paired us as first couple in mixed doubles matches and we paired ourselves in everything else. From the day I met Lindy I knew what it meant to fall hopelessly and irrevocably in love. She says it was the same for her. Within three months we were engaged. Her parents liked me, and my prospects in the firm were good. But Mrs van Vuuren wanted no hasty wedding.

'Get to know each other,' she said. 'You're both very young. Lindy is only twenty and you are just twenty-two. You've heaps of time.'

She was one of those heavy, rather masterful South African women with generations of Dutch blood visible in her bulk, her fair colouring, blue eyes and the same bright hair as her daughter's. Dr van Vuuren was an Afrikaner born and bred on a Cape fruit farm. He spoke English with the pleasant Afrikaans accent that is like a foreigner's. He was a big burly man with a thatch of thick brown hair, greying a little at the temples, and the sort of broad uncompromising face that you could respect and trust. Just right for a G.P. His eyes, with their long experience of seeing into the depths of human frailty and suffering, were both penetrating and compassionate. He too wanted us to wait a while before we got married. Lindy was their only child and he wanted to be sure we weren't making a mistake.

'My wife and I have old-fashioned views on matrimony,' he told me with that slight roll to the 'r' in matrimony and every syllable separate and complete as if to make the word more impressive. 'It must be for keeps.'

'It will be,' I said. 'There'll never be anyone for me but Lindy. I'll make her happy if it kills me.'

He smiled. 'Let's hope it won't do that. She's a good girl. She takes life a little too seriously, perhaps. That may be our fault. It's the way we've brought her up.'

'You've brought her up perfectly,' I said.

Lindy didn't want to wait any more than I did, but we agreed to put off our wedding for a few months more.

She had a job. She worked full time in a flower shop arranging the bowls and vases that people are always sending to one another at the Cape.

'It's the sort of work I can go on doing after we're married,' she said, 'but part-time, perhaps.'

We reckoned we'd wait at least a year or so before we started a family. Just to get on our feet financially. Personally, I thought we'd leave it longer than that. We were both so young. There'd be plenty of time. I didn't want children. I wanted Lindy. The children could come later.

When I think of our happiness then I think of a joy so rarefied that it is beyond description. They talk of the rapture of the deep or of space, a rapture incredible to man in his earthly element. Our explorations of our love were like that, revelations of bright alien worlds and a constant awareness of each other that was the solid axis of our whole existence. Our days and nights revolved round our love which touched and transformed the most trivial gestures, pervading every act of passion with a mystique in which bliss and anguish were indistinguishable. We cherished it as if we feared to lose it.

'We're too young for it – for all this feeling,' Lindy said once. 'It's too much for us.'

I was steeped in her innocence and sincerity. She was my girl, my woman, my young love. I tried to tell her so. There was a glitter on everything, the leaves of the trees, the sands beside the sea, the spears of grass our bare feet flattened those cool dewy nights when we tiptoed across the lawn to let her into her parents' house after a late party. The feel of her silky hair and her firm skin was imprinted upon my palms long after she had left me and her face lived within my eyelids sleeping or waking. I was mad about Lindy. I think I always will be.

Then one morning in my office the dream shattered. The sun shone across my desk, the sounds of Strand Street were loud and busy because it was hot and the window was open. The brunette from the typists' pool had just gone off with some work for me, the flirtatious sway of her hips vanishing through the open door. Then the coloured messenger who operated the lift came in.

'Mr Symes, there's a man named Jacobs insists on seeing you. A hunchback.'

'Insists?' I repeated, annoyed.

'He says you'll remember him.'

That was when my heart tumbled in my chest and sank down into my stomach the way it did when I dropped that glass.

'Oh, yes, Jacobs. Of course I remember. Tell him to come in.'

So he entered, soft-footed and purposeful. He shut the door behind him and crossed to my desk. There were no preliminaries.

'I have a letter for you, Master.'

He took it from the pocket of his shabby misshapen jacket and laid it in front of me – a grubby envelope addressed to Derek Symes, Esq. in a precise tidy hand I recognised. She had left occasional notes for me with the laundry.

I stared at it as if it were a snake, with my heart down there in my belly and my throat heavy and liquifying as if I might be sick.

'She told me to bring an answer.' His face was sly and stubborn, darker than I remembered it. He turned and moved high-stepping to the window and looked out while he waited for me to read what Veronica had written. I did so, dumb and shocked.

At last I addressed his deformed back. 'Come in an hour's time and I will give you a letter. I'm busy now.'

He looked at the clumsy watch on his wrist.

'At twelve o'clock, Master. When the gun goes.'

At noon every day the population of Cape Town sets

its watches and clocks by the boom of the midday cannon. I tried to grin at Jacobs but God knows what grimace twisted my face for he looked at me strangely. Expectantly.

'Yes,' I said. 'When the gun goes come back. I'll see you then.'

# 3

## JOHN BURFORD

---

*'Now was my chance to break it up'*

It was just after twelve when I had to take some papers to discuss with Derek Symes. Outside his office I ran into a little coloured dwarf who was muttering to himself. They say it's good luck to touch a hunchback, and if it is I hope Derek took advantage of his opportunity. He looked terrible when I went in. Normally he's a good-looking guy with a lively expression and the sort of smile that would charm a vulture off a carcass. But this particular morning he looked like the Blood Transfusion Service had bled him dry. He had his elbows on his desk and his head in his hands and when he glanced up at me his eyes were dead.

'You hung over?' I asked.

'I wish it were that,' he said.

'Can I help?'

He seemed to think for a bit, pressing his fingers hard against the tops of his eye-sockets. Then he said:

'Perhaps you can. I need advice most desperately.'

47

'Come to my place this evening. We can cook up a meal and you can give me the picture.'

'I'm going out with Lindy, but I can make an excuse. I must. Some client I've got to meet – anything. I can't face Lindy just now.'

He sounded sick.

'Do that then,' I said.

'Don't say a word to a soul. This problem is so goddamn confidential —' He broke off. 'What did you want, John?'

'Business. These Williamson papers.'

'Okay. Go ahead.'

He pulled himself together and we got down to Aston Brothers affairs. He has a good lucid brain and nailing him down to business helped. I wanted to take him out to lunch but he said no, he had some sandwiches, so we arranged to meet around six o'clock at my flat in Sea Point.

We ate very late because he began to pour the whole disastrous story out over our drinks. I filled his glass often enough to loosen up a few inhibitions, and eventually round ten o'clock we opened a can of soup and fixed ourselves sausages and eggs with hunks of toast. Then cheese and fruit and after that we drank some beer. The night was warm and we sat on the little balcony overlooking the sea and every now and again he covered his eyes as if the sight of the moon trail on the water was more than he could stand.

'You see' he said, 'it wasn't as if she was a *dark* coloured girl. In London you wouldn't think of her as coloured at all. You might wonder a bit because of that – exotic look – the eyes and the softness of her features. She could be Cypriot or Maltese except for the slant of those eyes and that's Eastern, not even African. I know the law here but I couldn't see it as wrong – what we were doing. It was less wrong somehow than if she'd been a girl of one's own sort. I can't live without sex, there has to be someone, and she was willing to take a chance. What was the harm? And now this!'

'Look,' I said. 'Aren't you making too much out of the whole thing? Hundreds of girls have illegitimate babies all the time.' But I saw the snags.

'Yes', he agreed bitterly. 'And anywhere else in the world you can make some sort of legal provision for the child and get something in writing – some sort of document – absolving you from further responsibility.'

'You can arrange to provide for Veronica's son. I can draw up an agreement.'

'But surely such an agreement would be an admission of criminal guilt. It could land us both in big trouble if anyone found out.'

'We can make a plan all the same. We can get round it somehow. I presume you don't want to be in touch with her personally.'

'Man, I daren't! You'll have to go up there for me.'

'That's okay. I can make a deal with Veronica.'

He began to pace about.

'Don't you see the ghastly fix I'm in? There's Lindy. You can't tell a girl like Lindy about this sort of thing, and what in hell would her old man say! My God, he'd sooner see me dead than married to his daughter if he knew. He's all for the Immorality Act, for keeping the white race pure and all that sort of stuff. There's no room in his philosophy for what I've done. God knows how we got caught – I suppose one of us was careless that last night.'

'Are you sure it's yours?'

'Veronica's honest. She's decent though you might find that hard to believe. There was no one else those months she was coming to my room. I'd swear to it.'

I made a mental note to check that. I took her letter out of my pocket and read it again. It was short and to the point. It made few claims, no emotional appeals at all:

Dear Derek,

My son – our son – was born last week. I have been out of a job for the last two months and I am short of cash. He must be fed and clothed. I will start work again soon but I need help to bring this boy up properly. Can you come and see me? I did not write to you before as I was afraid someone at the office might open the letter and I had no private address for you in Johannesburg. But when I read of your engagement in the paper I knew you were back. I don't want to make trouble for you but I must think of the child.

PS. I am sending this to your office with Jacobs. He can be trusted to deliver it to you personally. Please give him an answer.

Derek had answered: 'I will send somebody trustworthy to see you. I hope you are well.' No signature.

He lit a cigarette, his hand not quite steady.

'What I can't stand is beginning life with Lindy with something to hide. Her father knows my exact financial situation. If I've got to stump up a monthly allowance to Veronica how am I going to explain it?'

'Can't you say you have to allow your mother a certain amount? She's written to you and needs help —'

He laughed shortly.

'My parents are both dead – killed in a car crash two years ago – and I have no sisters and brothers. That's why I have a small private income. Without it I couldn't have asked Lindy to marry me.'

'We'll have to invent an old auntie. Leave it to me. I'll go and see this girl tomorrow.'

'I feel such a goddamn heel – to Lindy and to Veronica. You do a damn fool thing and you're landed with a child – another life – a responsibility that will outlive you, that will go on and on, a danger and a millstone, a secret I dare never share with Lindy.'

'Be your age,' I said. 'No life is an open book, but none! We all have something to hide, something that makes us prickle with shame every time we think of it. We've got to accept our secrets and keep them and shove them in the dark part of our minds. That's all there is to it.'

He looked at me then with his funny crooked grin and the little gold filling in a top tooth glinted.

'You too?' he asked.

'Me too. Everybody.'

'Want to tell?'

'That's one thing you have to learn not to do – not to talk in your cups or your sleep, or any other time. No confidence for confidence, see?'

He went off soon after that and I think the poor bastard felt better. But I was more worried than I cared to admit. Could this thing ever turn out to be a boomerang that might hit Lindy? A lot would depend on Veronica. What sort of girl was she?

Next day I plugged up to her home in District Six. I didn't go by car all the way. Too conspicuous. The 'tablecloth' poured over the face of the Mountain and the hot wind whistled down the steep narrow streets where coloured, Indian and Malay children romped and shouted. Some Chinese played a gambling game on a street corner.

The little villa was high up in an oasis of comparative calm opposite the schoolhouse and playing fields. It was sturdily built with a miniature front garden where a few petunias and zinnias battled against the south-easter. It was nearly six o'clock and the children had long since gone home or at all events they had left the precincts of the school. A stray dog sniffed round my ankles as I opened the wooden gate. It was right on the mountain-side and far below spread the bay and the city and the wide expanse of the Flats rolling away towards the northern mountain ranges.

There was a narrow covered stoep in front of the house and a man sat in one corner of it reading the evening newspaper. His thick wavy hair was greying and he wore spectacles, he had a grave thoughtful face and he did not smile as he rose to greet me.

'Mr Arendse?' I asked.

He folded the *Argus* and put it down on the stone seat.

'Yes,' he said. 'I am Luther Arendse. And your name, sir?'

'John Burford. I'm a lawyer, Mr Arendse, and I've come to see your daughter on behalf of my client.'

'Your client's name, Mr Burford?'

'I am not at liberty to tell you. But no doubt your daughter has mentioned it.'

He ran his hand up the back of his head and sucked in his breath. 'My daughter has not told me who the father of her son is. Does she expect you?'

'She expects me, but we have no appointment. I haven't met Miss Arendse before.'

I was determined to make my own position perfectly clear. He had looked at me with a shadow of suspicion.

'Will you come in. I'll call Veronica.'

He opened the front door into a narrow passage and led me into the front room on the left. Other doors evidently opened into bedrooms and the passage widened into the dining-room and kitchen quarters at the back. Someone was thrumming a guitar. The floors were covered with linoleum with here and there a rug. They smelled of polish. There were artificial flowers in an ornate vase and a large print of the Good Shepherd hung on the main wall. The bearded shepherd, complete with halo and crook, carried a black lamb draped over one arm. A pile of children's exercise books was stacked on an upright chair. Homework, I guessed.

'Do you mind if I smoke?'

'No,' said Mr Arendse. 'There's an ashtray on that small table by the sofa.'

He accepted a cigarette from me and as we lit up I heard her come in. She had a quick light step. When I glanced up and saw her slight figure and neat dark head

I knew what Derek had meant when he'd said 'In London you wouldn't know she was coloured. You'd wonder . . . exotic.' The eyes that met mine with interest were indeed oriental rather than African, light brown and brilliant. Cat's eyes really. She wore a simple cotton dress.

'Veronica, this is Mr Burford. He wants to talk to you.'

She acknowledged her father's introduction with a curt nod.

'Can Mr Burford talk to me alone?' she asked.

Mr Arendse drew himself up to his full height – maybe five foot six. I'm not much more myself. He answered his daughter in quiet dignified Afrikaans. It was the language of his home and the language in which he taught. In Afrikaans somehow his authority increased.

'I prefer to stay with you. Whatever Mr Burford has to suggest concerns all of us.'

She did not argue. She merely bowed her head. She too had dignity. I was impressed and relieved.

'Mr Burford, it's necessary to make some provision for my child.'

'That's why I'm here, Miss Arendse.'

'Please sit down,' said her father and swept the school books off the chair. He took off his spectacles, wiped them with a clean handkerchief and put them on again.

Veronica sat on the sofa, her long slender legs crossed, her father took the small upright chair and indicated an armchair for me with a gesture of his narrow almost feminine hand. I sat down. He looked at his daughter as he said:

'Veronica has her own ideas about everything. I think it's best that she should explain what she wants.'

I waited for her to speak in that soft husky but extraordinarily determined voice.

'I need a monthly sum – we can decide what's fair – to feed and clothe my son properly and I need a sewing-machine —'

'She's lost her job, of course, and she can't go back to it,' her father intervened. 'Her mother is dead and we have no one to leave the boy with. She must work at home.'

'I'm good at dressmaking. People in the flats used to get me to make things for them but I worked in their places and used their machines. I prefer it that way. It makes a change. But with the baby to consider it's different. I can let my customers know I'm here and they can come to me and I'll work here till I consider the boy is old enough to be left in the crêche. I won't leave him as a tiny baby. I have an old hand-machine that belonged to my ouma. But it's broken – finished. I need a new one. Electric, with a foot pedal and gadgets.'

'What would such a thing cost?'

'About a hundred and fifty rand.'

'That's a lot of money.'

'You don't have to pay it all at once.'

'You want it on the never never?'

She smiled suddenly and the effect on her face was astonishing. It grew lighter as if clouds had dispersed and I realized, with something like dismay, that this girl was not only intelligent but very attractive. She had quality. I began to sympathize with Derek and pulled up short.

'That's up to your client.' She stressed the word 'client' as if indulging an eccentricity. 'Let him pay whatever way suits him best so long as I have the machine. But he'd get a discount for cash.'

'That's one thing,' put in Mr Arendse, 'that is an essential thing. But, now when it comes to the monthly sum, how can we be sure it will not be discontinued before the boy is old enough to earn his own money? Can you draw up an agreement?'

'Mr Arendse,' I said, stubbing out my cigarette and helping myself to another – a bad habit but one I can't break when I'm nervous. 'You are right to wish to protect your daughter, but I'm sure you must see that your suggestion isn't feasible.'

He frowned and his eyes narrowed behind his spectacles. His thin face had set in a stubborn mould.

'We need some sort of guarantee.'

'Your daughter knows the father of her child, even if

you don't – and *the fewer people who know the better* – I think she must trust him.'

Mr Arendse made an impatient movement and Veronica sat very still and silent. Suddenly I rose.

'May I see the child?'

'He's asleep,' said Veronica.

'I won't wake him.'

'Come!'

She stood up and I followed her out of the front room and into a bedroom diagonally opposite it. It was furnished with an iron bedstead covered with one of those woven bedspreads. I think it was green or maybe blue. The curtains, partially drawn, were of the same material. There was a low dressing-table with a long mirror and two wings so that you could see yourself from various angles if you adjusted them and there was also a wardrobe and a small chest of drawers. It was clean and tidy like the girl herself in spite of a certain amount of infant paraphernalia here and there. On the bed was a sort of basket – I think you call it a carrycot – and from it came a slight snuffling noise such as puppies sometimes make. I recalled that this baby was pretty new.

She opened the curtains to give more light, then she turned back the pale blue blanket that covered the baby. Her lashes against her cheek were sweeping and her mouth had softened. Her whole face was soft and fluid as she bent over him.

'Look, then,' she said to me.

I stepped to her side and looked down at the tiny head. The baby lay on his back, one diminutive hand was outside the blanket, the nails surprisingly rosy. The thick fluff of hair on the little head was dark auburn and the smooth skin of the face was pale like mutton-fat jade. The features were tiny and delicately carved. With a shock I realized that I was staring into the face of a European baby. I could see no special likeness to Derek except the hair colour and perhaps in the finely carved nostrils, but then I never can spot resemblances in babies.

'His eyes are dark blue now,' she said. 'But they'll change. They'll probably be brown.'

Her father was standing in the doorway, pride and anger gathering in his near-sighted eyes.

'Life will be hard for him,' he said. 'He's too fair. It's better to be the same as the others. He'll never know where he really belongs and he's already classified as coloured because of his mother and me. Yet his white skin should entitle him to equal opportunities with other white children, but those he will never have because of his birth and his background.'

He moved into the room and put his dark thin hand over the child's.

'He'll be kept out of the best work by Job Reservation, the Immorality Act will see that he never marries a white girl and the Group Areas won't allow him to buy a house in a white district. He'll have to exist as one of us all his life – a second-class person with a second-class future, no matter what his individual capacity may be. There's no equality of opportunity in our country, as you know, Mr Burford. No equality at all – and look at that boy!'

The old sense of injustice and despair were in every true and bitter word. I had nothing to say. Veronica covered her child again and drew the curtains once more. We returned to the front room.

'I can offer you a glass of sherry,' said Mr Arendse more calmly.

'Thank you. I'd like that.'

He took glasses and a bottle of sweet brown sherry from a corner cupboard. He filled the three glasses and we resumed the seating pattern we had adopted before.

'About an agreement,' he persisted. 'You must see our point of view.'

'I do.' I put my finger between my collar and my neck as if to loosen my tie a bit, I could feel my Adam's apple rise and fall. 'But you must realize something too. Your daughter and my client are very vulnerable. I hate to say this, but the Immorality Act is rigorously enforced. Anything in writing would be incriminating for obvious reasons. If anybody cares to spill the beans both Miss Arendse and my client will go to prison. There'd be no fine, no chance of a reprieve. It would be iron bars – and what good would that do the baby?

You must let me work something out about an allowance and about the sewing-machine. We could perhaps
use Jacobs as a go-between where the money is concerned. He's reliable, I gather?'

'He's my cousin's husband,' said Veronica. 'He's
fond of my father and me. I can't believe he'd hurt us.'

'Will he keep his mouth shut?'

'I hope we can trust him,' said Mr Arendse. 'He
knows so much already we are in his hands.'

'I'll make a plan with my client,' I said. 'I'll be in
touch with you in the next few days, Mr Arendse. I see
you are on the telephone.'

'Yes,' he glanced at the instrument on a small
imbuia wood table. 'But it's urgent, don't forget. We
aren't rich people and Veronica needs work. She needs
money and the machine.'

'I understand.'

I finished my sherry and put down my glass. As I got
up to go they came with me to the door. Veronica's
father went down the steps of the high stoep to the
gate and as I was about to follow him she called me
back.

'Tell him' – she whispered – 'tell Derek the child is
a boy to be proud of —'

Her voice broke and those remarkable eyes were
swimming with tears.

'I won't forget.'

The sun was setting as I walked down the long

curving hill seething with its vigorous squalid life, its shops and markets and cafés, its shabby inhabitants – children pushing companions in a soap-box cart, a boy deliriously happy on one ancient roller skate, his friend on another, lads strumming guitars on street corners, girls in skin tight slacks or skirts, and here and there an old wrinkled man or woman sitting on a stool outside a dilapidated house watching the world go by. Watching me with some interest.

I was acutely conscious of the dark inquisitive eyes following me and it was a relief when a side street brought me back to the spot where I had left my car.

Along the de Waal Drive I stopped in one of the scenic bays to think. I scarcely saw the magical pattern of lights begin to prick the dusk. I saw the white baby and his mother with her acceptance of the situation, her claims on the father no more than seemed reasonable. I no longer doubted that it was Derek's child. I saw too Mr Arendse's bony embittered face, the tea-coloured skin stretched tight over high sharp cheekbones, the resentful eyes behind the cheap spectacles, and the tiny ears. He was a scholar and a thinker and he was right in fearing for the future of his too fair grandson.

But then another face rose to haunt me. Lindy's with its smoke-blue eyes and sensitive features. She was deeply in love with Derek and he with her. The thing, as far as Derek was concerned, had been over with Veronica before he had ever met Lindy. Yet, if her parents were to guess anything about it, they would undoubtedly bring all their weight to bear on Lindy to give Derek up. Would she? She belonged to the new generation which calls for a square deal for the under-privileged. She had joined the university student sit-in when the Government had vetoed the appointment of a certain African professor, she was prepared to fight for the rights of the underdog. But this was different. It was not theoretical but intensely intimately personal. Would she stand for that?

I found myself wanting to put her to the test – and seeking my own motives for feeling that way. I hadn't far to look. I knew them well enough! With a few unguarded words I could topple her dreams and ruin everything between her and Derek. Would that be best for her?

I put the car in gear and moved on. I'm not keen on soul searching. But I wasn't happy about this particular problem any more than Mr Arendse was. Too many people were closely concerned. Derek and Veronica and the two unconscious victims. The baby – and Lindy. Now was my chance to break it up before it was too late.

But I knew I never would.

# 4

## DEREK

*'A day of reckoning was at hand'*

John Burford was superb. He arranged everything. I simply made out a Banker's order to him and each month he shelled out a certain sum to Jacobs who called for it in John's office. I had no direct contact with either Veronica or the little hunchbacked go-between. We invented a destitute aunt in England to account for the decrease in my salary and Dr van Vuuren accepted this imaginary obligation without question. If anything, he seemed to respect my sense of duty to my dead father's non-existent sister. In many ways he is a simple man and certainly good-hearted, but he is narrow. The truth he would never have swallowed!

'When you get a raise in salary keep it quiet,' advised John. 'You can then murder your aunt.'

I grinned, but deep down I was appalled to realize that I wished both Veronica and her son out of the way. I daresay everybody has, at some time in the course of their lives, wished someone else dead. Really

64

*wished* it, I mean, not just said it. Never mind the reason. Maybe even someone they loved. How tortuous, how terrifying is the human mind! And how long lasting the consequences of our acts can be! That was what haunted me – the knowledge that I would have to live with this secret for always. And for the next eighteen years there would be a coloured child dependent on me for support. Say I were to be killed suddenly in an accident it would all come out. Veronica would claim on my estate in some way or another. I guessed that she would be ferociously protective towards this child. Sometimes I discussed these problems with John. It was a relief having someone to confide in.

'Be thankful for small mercies,' he said. 'In any other country her father might have tried to make you marry the girl. That certainly couldn't happen here! The all-embracing Immorality Act sees to that too. As to your being killed in an accident and the thing coming out, Veronica daren't risk a gaol sentence by staking a claim. So relax. She has to take certain chances and that's one of them.'

Once, however, he took a different line.

'Have you thought of putting the cards on the table? Telling Lindy everything and hoping she might understand.'

'Lindy's a South African. She fights her own ingrained prejudices but they are there. And she's devoted to her old folk. They'd consider it the blackest sin in every sense of the word. That attitude must inevitably brush off on Lindy.'

'Not necessarily. A lot of the young feel very differently from their parents. They don't like all this apartheid legislation. They struggle against it. The students are always demonstrating.'

'The English-speaking students. Yes. Not the Afrikaners, and the van Vuurens are Afrikaners. I can't risk losing Lindy.'

John shrugged and raised his eyebrows. He has a funny expressive face, with a square bellicose jaw and eyes that don't miss a trick. After he'd suggested telling Lindy the truth I played with the idea. When I was with her I'd find myself wondering about it. Theoretically she might be willing to make allowances for what I'd done but confronted with the fact? No, never.

I got used to my own sense of guilt after a while. Nothing happened to jolt it into life and it just lay there on my conscience, a quiescent shadow. I'm like that. I have a gift for pushing unpleasant facts underground. I dance on their grave.

A few months later we were married. That day, when Lindy was really mine, was the happiest of my life. John was our best man and when he said: 'Now it's my turn to kiss the bride', and made quite a meal of

66

it I suddenly thought, God, I believe the poor beggar's in love with her himself! Afterwards, when we were driving up through the mountains to Montagu for our honeymoon, I teased her about it. She gave me one of her long solemn blue-grey looks and said:

'After I met you there was nobody else.'

It didn't answer anything. And I remembered how John had talked about everybody having something to hide and a great flash of sexual jealousy blazed up in me. But I stamped it out. Who was I to start probing? Lindy was mine now and for ever, and that was all that mattered.

For the first year she kept on working part time in the flower shop. Then she said.

'Isn't it time we started a family?'

I wasn't so keen. It'd mean less luxury for us, less sport, less dancing.

'It's a big tie, having a family. Baby-sitters and all that sort of thing. It's a sacrifice.'

'It's one I want to make. Children – say, two – would be worth a sacrifice and we want to be young with them. It's more fun for the kids – and for the parents.'

Well, I believe that sort of decision is up to the woman. In the long run it's she who bears most of the heat and burden of the day.

But nothing happened. It hasn't happened yet. She seems to think I might be to blame. As if I didn't know only too well that I'm not! If it weren't for Lindy minding so much I wouldn't give a damn about the babies being slow to appear. We have a lovely little home and a good life and lots of friends.

Then I heard about this transfer to London for a couple of years and a sizeable raise in salary. Fine. I told John about it at once.

'I'll miss you both,' he said. 'But it sounds great. Congrats. And surely now – with that raise – it's the time to kill your aunt.'

'How do I do it? I'm not experienced in creating and demolishing aunts.'

'You tell Lindy you've had a letter from her solicitors. I can cook one up if you like.'

'Not necessary. I'll just tell her.'

But I didn't get around to it then. That was the evening I mixed the celebration martini and Lindy said, 'That sewing-girl – Veronica Arendse —' and I knew that somehow, some way, a day of reckoning was at hand.

# 5

## LINDY

---

*'I had a curious feeling that I fascinated her'*

When Veronica came next day, I said, when we'd finished the fitting:

'Things have changed since yesterday. When my husband came home yesterday evening he told me we were not just going to London for a few weeks. We are to go for two years.'

She was tacking a seam and she stopped her work to stare at me. Her eyes had widened and her lips parted.

'Are you pleased?' she asked.

'Very. It should be interesting to live in London and I want to travel in Europe too. I've been once with my parents, but this will be different.'

'To travel! To see other parts of the world where all men are equal. I should like that.'

I said briskly, 'I doubt if you'd find all men equal anywhere in the whole world. That's a dream and a theory.'

'At least there are people who dream it —'

'And try to put the theory into practice. You're

right, Veronica. There's hope where there's right thinking. It's a start. As a matter of interest, do you think the Bantu are equal to the coloured people?'

She laughed and there was that sudden brightening of her face which I had noticed before – as if the sun shone on it.

'They're different. They're brought up in tribes. In tribal law they can have several wives. When our girls marry Natives and go with them to their countries in the north they aren't happy. Our girls are brought up to think like Europeans. I don't say we're better than Natives. I say we aren't the same, we're more like whites. We don't carry heavy burdens in baskets or basins on our heads.' Her eyes darkened. 'Sometimes we carry them in our hearts.'

'You coloureds belong with us,' I agreed. 'We in the Cape know that. But our Government is mostly of the Transvaal.'

'The Government intends us to develop along our own lines. So they say. But our lines should be white. All the same, my father says we must do as they tell us, we will have our own towns and town councils, and, in time, a sort of shadow parliament. He says these things will teach us to grow up and to think for ourselves and learn what's what. It will prepare us for the day when the blacks in the north rise against the whites. That day the whites at the Cape will need us and we'll need them! We don't want to be ruled by blacks any more than they do. Perhaps that day the whites will get together with the coloureds – because they'll have to if they are to survive at all.'

I realized anew that she was the daughter and the granddaughter of schoolmasters, thinking men. Discussions must go on in her home constantly. She was probably echoing her father's point of view when she let herself go in talking to me but it sounded convincing.

'Anyway, all that's a long way off,' she went on. 'In the meantime we have no equality of opportunity. The best jobs are reserved for whites – like the best beaches and group areas. A white principal doing the same work as my father under much easier conditions gets better pay. If a white woman was sewing for you, Mrs Symes, you would have to pay her a great deal more than you give me.'

She was right, of course, and she was knocking the nail on the head with every word she spoke, but grievances are always boring and I was getting restless.

'If you're satisfied with what I give you, Veronica, you might be able to come to me for two more days before we sail.' I spoke rather curtly.

'I'd like to,' she said with a quick smile. 'When would you need me?'

'Early in June. We leave about the end of June.'

'I go to Mrs Seymour for two days the first week in June. I could ask her to spare me to you.'

'She won't be pleased.'

Ann Seymour was always having garments made or altered. She was mad on clothes and she wore them well for her age – though no one knew quite what that was. Somewhere round sixty perhaps. She had teenage grandchildren who visited her from time to time.

'Mrs Seymour is your friend,' said Veronica as if that simplified everything.

I raised my eyebrows and we both laughed.

'I'll ring her. In the circumstances she might be willing. But you know how she is.'

'I'd like to help you out,' persisted Veronica.

I had an unreasonable feeling that, in some way or other, I fascinated her. I was conscious of her interest in me reaching out across the gulf between our ways of life like the tentacles of an octopus, seeking, flexing, stretching, exploring the element in which we both existed so differently, as if at the first touch she would be enabled to close in upon me and possess me. Absurd. But it was there all the time, the awareness of an abnormal, growing significance in our relationship. Relationship? How could there be any such thing between her and me? The only point of contact was her quick competence with her needle.

'She's a coloured lady,' Ann Seymour had said of her. It was a favourite term of hers in describing the people who worked for her. 'The little man who upholsters my chairs, Lindy, he's so nice. Very respectful and well-mannered, a real coloured gentleman.' She was familiar and yet gracious with these people. She'd drink a cup of tea with them and joke and ask them about their families and learn a great deal about them in her slow, pleasant intensely human way. Being a widow she gets lonely and needs conversation. I made up my mind to ask her a bit more about Veronica. Oddly enough, I didn't have to ring her up, after all. She dropped in during the morning and we had a cup of coffee by the fire in the living-room. Minnie, lumbering, clumsy and good-natured, limped in and put down the tray for us. Ann greeted her with an understanding smile.

'Good morning, Minnie. This damp weather gets into your bones, doesn't it?'

'Ja, Meddem, it's terrible – this rheumatics! It's in my knees this morning.'

'You and I know about these things, Minnie. Your Madam doesn't. She's too young. What do you do for it?'

'Horse liniment. I smear it on an' rub it in. My brother has a horse what's gone in the knees. This smeergoed fixes up the beast so my brother says to me, "You try it, Minnie, an' you'll keep on your feet".'

'That's splendid and I've got some tablets with me that'll help you too. Get a saucer and I'll give you some.'

Minnie hobbled off to fetch a saucer and Ann winked at me.

'Just cheap aspirin, my dear. I always carry it. You know how they crave a tablet – any damn tablet. Just give them something and faith does the rest.'

She put nine tablets in the saucer and Minnie's black eyes lit up.

'One after meals. That, combined with the horse dope, should put you right. The trouble with us is we aren't as young as we were.'

When Minnie had returned to the kitchen Ann said:

'I really came about Veronica. I knew she was here today and I want a word with her. She's supposed to give me two days the first week in June but I shan't need her. I'm flying up to Pretoria then – just for a fortnight. I can fix her up with Hope van der Spuy —'

'No, please don't! I need her at that time.'

I told her about Derek's new job and she was delighted for our sakes.

'Then we'll fix that up with Veronica today,' she said finally. 'Of course you'll need things for the ship.'

'Veronica's an odd girl. She has a sort of quality – grace – and she's highly intelligent with a king-size chip on her shoulder. What's her story, Ann?'

'Her story, who knows? These folk have the most dramatic private lives. All I can tell you about her is that her father, Luther Arendse, is a highly respected and well-known schoolmaster – principal of a school as

74

his father was before him. There's a strong scholastic background, an interest in politics and in the advancement of the coloured people. You must have read some of Luther Arendse's stories and articles in the *Cape Times*. Bitter stuff sometimes but well expressed. What you call her quality – her physical grace and gentle speech – comes from her mother, I imagine. Her mother was one of the leading lights in the Eoan Dramatic Group until she died last year. She taught her daughter deportment and speech training.'

'Why isn't she married?'

'Hard to suit, I'd say. But there's a child, I believe. A boy. Hope van der Spuy has seen him – says he's as fair as any white child. Rather pathetic, really.'

'You get that,' I said. 'The throwbacks can be black as your hat or lighter than many of our friends. It's just a matter of genes. She has a steady, I suppose.'

'She swears she has no boy-friend. Most unnatural.'

John Burford came in that evening about five. He often turns up unexpectedly, especially if he's been playing tennis over our side of the Peninsula. However, this time tennis had nothing to do with it.

'I've left Derek at a conference,' he said. 'He'll be back late.'

'What sort of late?'

'Oh, not too bad. Sevenish, I guess.'

It was pouring then, coming down in torrents.

'Make yourself at home,' I said. 'I've got to take my sewing-woman down to the Main Road. She'd be drenched to the skin in this downpour. I'll just get her to the bus-stop and then I'll be right back.'

'I'll take her,' he offered. 'No trouble.'

I hesitated. These days it isn't very wise for a young man to be seen driving with a coloured girl beside him. But then Veronica didn't look really coloured at a passing glance and in this pelting rain even the most hawk-eyed policeman would hardly be likely to notice her. It's only when a car's suspiciously parked with a couple in it that they start prying.

'Well, thanks,' I said. 'If you really don't mind. It'll save me getting the car out.'

So I went into the sewing-room where she'd already folded her work neatly away.

'There's only this blouse still to do,' she said. 'I'll tackle it when I come next month. I'll leave it here on top of the work basket.'

I paid her and we agreed on the date she was to come again.

'Lucky it suited Mrs Seymour.' She smiled as she put on her coat and tied a waterproof kerchief over her hair. She glanced at the window. 'Cats and dogs! I may have to swim for it.'

'A friend of ours – Mr Burford – will take you to the bus-stop. He's waiting.'

It may have been a trick of the light but it seemed

to me that the healthy glow went out of her face, leaving it greenish like putty. She collected herself visibly.

'That's kind of your friend. Good-bye, Mrs Symes.'

I led her through the living-room and on to the front porch where John was waiting.

'This is Veronica Arendse,' I said.

'Good evening,' said John very brusquely.

The storm made it dark and she ducked her head and ran to the car. He opened the door for her and she tucked herself into the passenger's seat next to the driver's. Next moment he was at the wheel, the windscreen wipers were working, and they were away. He was gone a great deal longer than I'd expected. When at last he came back I was quite upset.

'What on earth happened? I'd given you up.'

'I took her back to District Six. There was no shelter at the bus-stop. She'd have been drowned.'

'That was nice of you, but it wasn't necessary —'

'I thought it was.'

He bit off the words and I looked at him, puzzled. He seemed annoyed.

'I'm sorry, John. I didn't mean to impose on you. Have a drink. Whisky and water?'

'Make it strong – to keep the cold out.'

He warmed his back at the fire and I mixed his drink. I know his tastes as well as I know Derek's. He took the tumbler from me and raised it.

'Congrats. Derek told me about the new job today. Lucky blighter.'

'It'll be a wonderful experience to live in London. I mean to find a flat somewhere in Chelsea. I adore Chelsea. Or South Kensington maybe.'

'Your parents'll miss you. So will we all.'

'Mummy was here to tea this afternoon. She hates our going but she knows it's the best thing for us.'

'It is,' he agreed. 'Oh, believe me, my dear dear Lindy, it is the very best possible thing for you both.'

Then he did a strange thing. He put down his glass and took mine from me and put that down too. I felt his arms go round me and he held me very tight and very still with his cheek close against mine – we are much of a height. He didn't even kiss me, just held me like that for a long quiet moment as if he couldn't bear to let me go. I rested against him.

'Lindy,' he whispered at last, 'God bless you and keep you safe – always.'

I shivered as I drew away from him.

'Is something wrong?'

'I don't know,' he said.

Then Derek came in and I couldn't ask John anything more.

# 6

## JOHN BURFORD

---

*'Nothing is ever finished'*

When Derek had telephoned me that afternoon he'd sounded excited, and worried too. He'd told me about the new job first. That was cause for rejoicing. Then he'd dropped the bombshell.

'That girl – Veronica Arendse – she's in my house right now – sewing for Lindy. She came yesterday and she's there again today, and Lindy wants her for two days next month.'

'Perhaps she didn't realize Lindy was your wife. Perhaps she was just recommended to a Mrs Symes —'

'You know Veronica! She's too clever to make that sort of mistake. She must have known. She has some ulterior motive. Frankly I'm worried. Scared, if you want the truth.'

'I'll go to your place at once – while she's still there. I'll see what I can find out.'

'Do that. And tell Lindy I'll be late. I'm taking no chances on meeting Veronica. It's nearly five now. You might just catch her.'

79

The rain and Lindy's kind heart had made the rest easy. I gave Veronica a lift home. I hadn't seen her since we'd finally agreed on the settlement about the sewing-machine and the monthly allowance for the boy, Alexander – Lex, she called him.

'Did you expect to see me, Mr Burford?' she asked as we drove away from Lindy's house.

'Yes. Mr Symes rang me up and told me you were working in his home. Why?'

'Why not?'

'You know very well why not.'

'One customer recommends me to another. Mrs Seymour told Mrs Symes about me and she was determined to get hold of me.'

'You needn't have gone. I'm sure you have all the work you can reasonably undertake.'

'This is not the way to the Main Road and my bus-stop, Mr Burford.'

'I'm taking you all the way home – along the de Waal Drive. That way we'll have time to talk.'

'It's the peak hour,' she reminded me rather unnecessarily. 'You don't want to be seen driving a coloured girl.'

'Never mind what I want or don't want. What interests me at this moment is why you've oiled your way into Mr Symes's home.'

It wasn't too slow going towards Cape Town. The commuters were all coming the other way, back to their homes in the southern suburbs. Their cars were nose to tail for miles, wipers working, everybody concerned with their own problems, curbing their impatience. We slid past them fast and easily. I kept my eyes on the road but I felt her silence grow hostile.

'I have my reasons,' she said defensively.

I didn't look at her face but I could see it. Sullen. My God, how sullen the coloureds can look when they're fed up! Dark as the inside of a Dutchman's hat. Their skins – their ever-vulnerable skins – darken. They're a chameleon lot. Their emotions are the twigs that change their colour – light when they're happy, dark when they're angry, and grey when they're sad or frightened. She was angry, not frightened, now. She was dangerous. I felt a sort of purpose emanating from her as she sat beside me. We'd turned up past the wild life sanctuary and the Hospital bend and the pine woods were swaying and rocking in the storm. But the rain had lessened. Another five minutes and we'd be at her home. The bay had come into view, lashed into a fury of white waves.

'You remember the way to my father's house?' she asked. 'Up this turn on the left, then right.'

'I remember.'

So we were there.

Quite suddenly the rain stopped and a brilliant golden shaft of light burst out over the seaward side of Lion's Head. The school playing-fields were wet and green, gilded by the evening glow. I drew up outside the villa.

'Listen,' I said. 'What reasons can you have for this intrusion? What's done is done and what's finished is finished.'

'What's done is done,' she said in a tense husky voice. 'But nothing is ever finished. Never, never, never!'

She opened the door and got out and stood by the little wooden gate. I jumped out and lifted the catch and pushed the gate inwards. As I did so a child came scampering down the short garden path and hurled himself into her wide flung arms. He was a sprite of a boy and the last of the light made a furnace of his auburn curls. She turned to me.

'This is Lex – my son. He's getting on for four now. Quite tall for his age.'

I looked into the mischievous, intelligent black eyes of the little boy and said, 'Hullo Lex, hoe gaan dit?' and he grinned as he answered, 'Baie goed, meneer.' There wasn't a small gold filling in the upper row of milk teeth revealed by the wide smile and the eyes were clear and unflecked by amber speckles, but the paternity of Lex Arendse was stamped upon his features beyond dispute. I felt my heart contract.

'Your reasons?' I said to his mother. 'Once more I ask you why you should insinuate yourself into the home of Mrs Symes.'

Now that I saw her more closely I realized that the

girl I had last seen soon after the birth of her son had developed and hardened into a young woman of considerable character and determination. She was following some star of her own. She looked tenderly down at the laughing boy and then defiantly at me.

'It's simple enough, Mr Burford. There is only one reason. I want to know Mrs Symes. I want to know what sort of woman Derek Symes has married. Everything about her home and herself. Everything.'

'Why?'

'That's my business.' She took the child's hand in hers. 'And Lex's. Come Lex, we must go in. It's cold out here.' She turned to me. 'Thanks for the lift, Mr Burford. Good-bye.'

So there was an ulterior motive as Derek had guessed. But what – exactly what? I thought about it all the way back to Lindy's home. Only one thing was clear. Lindy was going to be dragged into this mess. Veronica meant to use Lindy.

The front door was unlocked as it always is when she's in and I let myself in without ringing the bell.

She stood up with her back to the fire as I came in and put out her hands to me. She looked anxious, a little frightened.

'What on earth happened?' she wanted to know.

I explained that I'd given Veronica a lift right home and not just to the Main Road. She mixed a drink for me and for herself and began to relax. She was happy about the new transfer to London. I only wished it could be sooner. I wanted to protect her from God alone knew what. I kept thinking, Lindy, my Lindy, what are they going to do to you between them? If I were a man who knew how to pray I would have prayed for her then. As it was, I followed an impulse too strong to resist. I took her in my arms and held her close, feeling the pliant body, the firm silky cheek against mine, and the trusting way she pressed against me – not sexy, but as if she too were afraid and in need of my strength. I wasn't making love to my friend's wife. I was trying to tell her without words that if ever she needed me I was there, an ally to pit against the intangible forces that were gathering against her.

Perhaps she wasn't even aware of them. I had read a sinister message into Veronica's words. It may be that instead of giving Lindy comfort I was infecting her with my own deep disquiet.

# 7

## LINDY

*'You're crying for the moon'*

As Derek had said, there was no difficulty in finding tenants prepared to pay a high rent for the house. Everybody is crazy about these converted Chelsea cottage areas. I suppose that's the sort of thing that'll happen to District Six when the coloureds are re-settled in the new towns on the Flats.

Veronica came for the two days she'd promised me and she helped me pack my trunk for the voyage. How quick and neat she was with her small olive hands, creating order out of a turmoil of sports and evening wear.

'There,' she said. 'Now everything is ready. When do you leave this house?'

'We go to my father's place the day after tomorrow and we'll finish the pack-up from there. It's not far. Wynberg.'

'Dr van Vuuren's?'

'You know my father?'

'I know of him. A friend of mine is gardener to Mrs

Waldon and when Dr van Vuuren goes to see the
mistress he sees the gardener too. My friend has a bad
heart but Dr van Vuuren has given him some wonderful tablets for his pains. Your father is kind.'

'I'm glad he was able to help your friend.'

I paid her what I owed her.

'It's half-past five and you're late,' I said. 'Shall I
drive you to the bus-stop or would you rather walk as
it's such a lovely evening?'

It was fresh and crisp with the scent of damp deep
drifts of oak leaves in the air and somewhere a garden
fire. 'If you don't mind, I'll wait in the kitchen,' she
said. 'My cousin's husband, Mr Jacobs, is coming to
fetch me in his car. He's bringing my little boy. Mr
Jacobs is a dwarf but he manages to drive. He has the
pedals of his car built up.'

That was the first I had heard of her son from
Veronica. But now I remembered that Ann Seymour
had mentioned a little boy. 'As fair as any white child –
rather pathetic.'

'Of course,' I said. It was Minnie's day out and she
had left us a cold supper. There wasn't any cooking for
me to do. Derek had said he'd be back by six.

'Your sewing-woman will have gone by then, won't
she?' he'd asked.

'Goodness, yes. She's supposed to go at five.'

But at six she was still there, reading the morning
paper at the kitchen table when I went in to get ice out

of the fridge and put out a drink tray. She looked up and smiled without rising.

'I expect my cousin's husband has got caught up in the traffic out of Cape Town.'

She didn't seem concerned but there was something odd about her attitude, something I couldn't fathom. She didn't offer to help me – not that there was anything much to do, only the ice, water, tonic and soda – she had, in a curious way, taken possession of the kitchen and I felt that there she intended to stay no matter how late her relation and her child might be.

'Mr Symes is late too,' she remarked.

'Not particularly. He practically never gets home before six.'

The smile was still on her lips but it had not touched her eyes.

'I should like to see him again,' she said.

I stood stock still, the tray in my hands, frozen by a totally unfamiliar insolence in her tone.

'*Again?* But you've never met my husband!'

'You'd be surprised.'

She leaned back on the little wooden chair, tipping up the front legs slightly.

The kitchen door was ajar and I walked silently through it into the dining-room, trying not to show that my knees had turned to jelly. I got whisky and gin out of the cupboard automatically and set the tray on the table in the living-room. I heard the

tradesmen's bell ring and Veronica's voice saying
something in Afrikaans, a man's mumbled reply, a
child's high treble and the closing of the kitchen door.
Almost simultaneously Derek came in with his usual
buoyant stride and in another moment he'd put down
his brief-case and I was in his arms.

He kissed me lightly, ruffled my hair with his cheek
and then held me away from him, his hands on my
shoulders. He was frowning, his hazel eyes worried.

'Lindy! You're shivering. What the hell's up?'

'I don't know,' I whispered. 'I simply don't know.'

He pushed me into a chair and stooped down to put
a match to the fire. The sticks crackled and it blazed up.
He added coal and a few fircones.

'You're cold as ice, honey. Why didn't you light the
fire earlier?'

'Veronica's still here. She wants to see you. She
seems to think she knows you, but she's never told me
that before.'

His gay irregular features stiffened as he rose and
faced me. The fire chattered to itself and we stared at
each other, speechless, threatened by God alone knew
what.

'What did Veronica tell you?' he said at last.

The cold that had impregnated my whole being
pierced my heart and I shuddered.

'Nothing. She just said she wanted to see you again.
*Again*, Derek. Why *again*?'

'Where is she?'

'In the kitchen. There's a man with her – and a child.'

He turned towards the kitchen but I stopped him before he reached the dining-room.

'No!'

My numbness had thawed into panic. But before I could move, the kitchen door opened and closed and Veronica came alone across the dining-room and into the living-room, brushing past Derek with her sleek black head held high. She was wearing that skin-tight skirt of hers and the cherry-red sweater with the polo neck. Everything about her was aggressive, the expression on her face, the thrust of her breasts, the way she made fists of her hands as she halted and took a stand in front of us both. Derek had moved swiftly to my side as if to guard me from harm.

'What do you want, Veronica?' he said in an icy voice that matched this new hard inflexible face I had never seen before.

'I want your wife to know the truth.'

'Why?'

'I have very good reasons – the best in the world. It's not for my sake I am doing this to you.'

Their gaze was locked. I could feel their wills wrestling although they stood so still confronting each other – she, desperate with the force of her intention, and he unyielding in his determination to resist her at any cost. I believe that in moments of great danger a human being can achieve unnatural calm. This happened to me now. The cold foreboding, followed by quick panic, was dissipated by a sense of inevitability. I didn't stand up because my body was still weak but my mind was clear and objective as if it were the mind of an onlooker.

'What is the truth you want me to know, Veronica?'

A long sigh escaped her and she stared down at the carpet. That muscle was twitching under her left eye. I could see it jump. Her eyes were set shallow in her face.

'I have a son by your husband, Mrs Symes.'

I was glad to be sitting down but my voice was steady. The little white boy?

'When . . . when was this child born?'

'Nearly four years ago. Before you were married.'

I looked at Derek for denial or confirmation.

'Lindy,' he said, the muscles of his throat so taut that I could see them standing out like ropes above his collar. 'When I met you the thing with Veronica had been over for months. It was over when I left Three Anchor Bay and went to Johannesburg, before I even knew you. I never saw her again after I left Cape Town that time. I swear it. I had no idea she was expecting a child. I never intended or wished to resume my . . . relationship with Veronica. It was only after our engagement was announced in the paper that she sent

me a letter to say a child had been born. Even then I
didn't see her.'

'What did you do about this child?'

I was outside myself, an inquisitor unrelated to Lindy
Symes but fiercely interested. Deeply shocked.

'I got John Burford to make a suitable financial
arrangement for me. He paid Veronica a monthly
allowance through the agency of a family connection of
hers, a hunchback night-watchman called Danie
Jacobs.'

'So John was in this too.' My feeling of betrayal
deepened. 'How many people know about Veronica
and . . . your child?'

Veronica answered quickly.

'Only Danie Jacobs and Mr Burford. Even my own
father doesn't yet know the name of my son's father.
I think he doesn't want to know. But soon he will have
to be told.'

'If the financial arrangement was satisfactory why
have you come into our home and forced this knowledge upon me?' I had to know her reason. There was
something serious behind this revelation.

'It was necessary. First I had to get to know you.
What I learnt was good. So it was necessary.'

'You know that if this information gets out you and
my husband will be prosecuted and sent to prison.
That is the law of our land. How do you know I won't
go straight to the police?'

'You love your husband.'

'I did,' I said.

I heard Derek groan.

'Did you come here to break up my marriage?' he asked Veronica.

She shook her head and gulped.

'Then what is it you want?' he demanded.

She flung back her shoulders and her brilliant almond eyes caught and held mine.

'I want you to adopt my son, Mrs Symes – your husband's child.'

'You must be mad!'

'He could pass for white,' she declared proudly.

'My wife is right. You're crazy, Veronica.'

She turned on Derek angrily.

'Why do you say that?'

'For God's sake be sensible! If we were to adopt a child here everybody would know about it. My parents-in-law would have a thousand questions to ask. Adoption isn't just a matter of taking a child into your house like a stray dog or cat. It's a legal procedure. Your boy is known in your neighbourhood. You can't just make him disappear from there. And we'd have to account for him here. In any case, why the devil should we even contemplate such lunacy?'

'He's not like other children,' she said stubbornly. 'He's special. My father says he has intelligence far above the average. In the white world he could have a

splendid future. Here there are ceilings, always
ceilings! Never never can you say of a coloured person
'the sky's the limit'. Repressive laws hold us back. My
father says Lex should be brought up white with every
opportunity.'

'Then emigrate! I'll help you. Raise him in Canada –
some other country —'

'I love this country,' she cut in simply. 'The mountains, the sea and the sun are ours as well as yours. Why
must we leave our land? All I want is a real fair chance
for my son – *here*.'

'It isn't possible – even if we were willing,' I said.
'You know that. You're crying for the moon.'

As if she saw a chink of weakness in what I had said,
she leaned forward, plunging after an invisible
advantage, her face intent and brooding.

'I have a plan. I've thought about this day and night
for months, longer than that! Ever since Lex went to
the crêche and proved that he was brighter than the
others. That was why I wanted to come and work for
you, Mrs Symes, and get to know you. Then Mrs
Seymour introduced me and it was easy. When I knew
you were going to England for two years, it all
seemed as if it might work out. It was like fate.' She
clasped her hands and wrung them. 'I'd go to prison
for this child if it would help! I'd do anything for him.
I'd even give him up – and that is the hardest thing of
all —' She choked and broke off.

'What was your plan?' I heard the coolness of my own voice and wondered at it.

'Does it matter?' cut in Derek, impatient. 'The whole thing's impossible. Mad.'

'Your plan, Veronica?' I persisted.

'When you are settled in London I'll fly there with Lex. I'll need money for that. My father will help me, so can you. I'll leave him there with you and come back. I'll tell my friends I've left him with an English family for adoption. It'll be true. Mr Symes has a British passport, he can adopt Lex. It can be done in England. And when you come back in two years time with a boy nearly six years old no one will guess his true parentage. I swear that I will never try to make myself known to him. Never, never, never. But at least I'll know what's happening to him – I'll be able to watch him become a man of importance, a white man —'

'And when he grows up and marries and has children – what then?' snapped Derek brutally. 'This is still South Africa. What happens when your man of importance fathers a coloured child on a white wife?'

'We are light skinned in my family. His children will pass.' She pouted, her lips thickening.

'So you hope. But you know full well how it can be. The dark strain is strong.'

She tossed her head in exasperation.

'We can't look ahead down the years and the centuries. All I'm asking is that this boy gets a chance here and now in your world where he can go ahead, and not in mine where there is a wall at the end of every street.'

Her colour had heightened. She was flushed as if she had applied rouge to her cheeks. Suddenly she ran across the room and called out in a loud commanding tone.

'Danie Jacobs, bring Lex here!'

The kitchen door flew open and a grotesque hunch-backed dwarf, grinning from ear to ear and holding a neatly dressed boy by the hand, came into the room with a peculiar soft high-stepping gait.

'Good evening, Mr Symes,' he said politely, and Derek nodded, his face ghastly.

The boy broke free of the hunchback and rushed to his mother as if overcome with the strangeness of his surroundings.

She went down on one knee and smoothed his copper hair with a gentle palm. She gave his pale blue pullover a little tug. He had a shirt and tie under it and she straightened the tie. He had grey shorts and socks to match his pullover.

'Don't be silly and shy,' she said in Afrikaans, and added in English 'Say good evening to Mr and Mrs Symes.'

She smiled at him in reassurance, and, indeed, her

face had regained its light attractive look as if the sight of the boy had restored her own confidence.

I rose and put out my hand.

'Come to me, Lex. Maybe I can find you a sweetie – 'n lekker.'

Till then I had only really seen the back of his head but now he turned and grinned in happy anticipation.

Derek tightened his grip on my shoulder and I felt him tense as the child looked at us and moved forward cautiously on sturdy legs. Rising four. No longer quite a toddler. At sight of his face my heart leapt up into my throat.

Lex was, without exception, the most beautiful child I have ever seen. The copper hair, only slightly curly, gleamed with the same racehorse sheen as Derek's, the features were carved out of old ivory, the nostrils delicate and complicated like my husband's and the little boy had the same trick of expanding them in moments of excitement such as this. His round cheeks were faintly rosy and his mouth, parted in a smile, showed the pearly baby teeth. His eyes were unforgettable – large, almond, moistly black and sparkling. Only the eyes betrayed the dark side of his ancestry. Although they were mischievous and merry now I knew that in repose they would hold the melancholy expression of his race.

He put his chubby dimpled hand into mine and I rose and moved out of the shelter of Derek's arm. It was as if the child and I launched out together under the eyes of his parents and the dwarf who stood in the shadows. We went across to the tallboy and I opened the drawer in which I keep the boiled sweets I often like to suck now that I have given up smoking. He had to stand on tiptoe to see into it.

'Lekkers!' he exclaimed and laughed with glee.

I took the lid off the tin and he thrust an eager little hand into it and helped himself to several.

'Put those in your pocket,' I said in Afrikaans, 'and now pass the tin round to your Ma and your friend. Mr Symes doesn't like them.'

He did as he was told and gave the tin back to me.

'Baie dankie, Missus,' he said, as I closed the drawer on it. Then he took a sweet from his pocket and began to suck it.

Veronica had slipped hers into her bag and I knew that she would save it for Lex. The hunchback had tucked his into his cheek and was evidently enjoying it.

Derek, who, in spite of himself, had been profoundly moved by the first sight of his son, was saying in a gentler tone than he had used yet:

'Veronica, we must have time to think. You are asking us to take a very big decision. A child's whole future is at stake. So is my wife's. It may be that she won't want to stay married to me after this. We must have a few days to think. Then I will ask Mr Burford to go and see you. Don't hope too much.'

The boy had gone to his mother, but although he pressed against her skirt, the great dark eyes were fixed on me as if he could read my thought. What I had failed to do this coloured girl had done triumphantly. She had given my husband a perfect son.

# 8

## DEREK

---

*'We'd been bulldozed into a false position'*

When they had gone – Veronica and the boy and the hunchback – I poured a drink for Lindy and one for myself in silence. The thing I had dreaded ever since my engagement to Lindy had happened. But it was more shocking and more far-reaching than I could have imagined in my worst nightmares. If only the child had been frankly and unmistakably coloured none of this would have arisen. As it was, Veronica was clearly determined to make us responsible for his future. She'd go to any lengths to 'give him his chance'. Her 'white child' was not going to grow up in an atmosphere of frustration and violence -- not if she could help him to cross the colour line. On her side of the line too many are ready to stab, rob and rape at the drop of a hat. Those are the bad ones, of course, and the decent ones like the Arendse family are the victims as often as not. Find me a coloured person who hasn't had close contact with crime. Some way or another, evil is for ever on their doorsteps. It is born of viciousness and despair and even those who rise above it have none the less brushed shoulders with the devil.

In allowing myself – a stranger to South Africa – to become involved with Veronica, I'd screamed out for trouble and God knows I'd got it.

It was Minnie's night out. We were alone – my beloved Lindy and I. What could we say to one another? What could we do? Through me she'd been dragged into something infinitely menacing. Somehow Veronica intended to thrust this boy upon us. She'd said that she would go to prison for her son if necessary. She was capable of doing just that – of blackmailing me by threatening to go to the authorities and confessing everything in the slender hope of getting the boy classified as white. She could ruin me – lose me my job as well as my friends, my freedom and my wife. Make no mistake about that! The van Vuurens would somehow make it impossible for Lindy to stay with me if such a scandal broke, even if she were willing.

'Lindy,' I said. 'What can I say? What can I do?'

She stood with her back to the fire, her face in shadow, her hair a halo of gold, shoulders drooping, her long appealing neck bent. Almost as if she bowed to fate. Yet I knew that she had matured in the past hour. She had neither wept nor stormed. I don't know what I expected. Recriminations? Disgust? An end to our marriage? More than likely. Instead she plunged straight at what, to her, was the heart of the matter.

'Now I know why you wouldn't go to a doctor. Why should you? The fault was mine and you knew it.'

She has a voice of great beauty – soft and very clear with filaments of light in it. When I hear her on the telephone I am aware of her vibrant quality. It's immensely expressive, and, strangely, now it carried little reproach. But it was dead. The light was out.

'How can you forgive me? I ought to have had the courage to tell you everything before we were married. But if I had you'd have broken with me and married John Burford instead. It might have been better so. He's always adored you. And then you'd never have been mixed up in this sordid mess. He's only mixed up in this problem for your sake.'

'I loved you. I love you still. Perhaps if you tell me everything now – how it all happened – I may be able to understand.'

I took heart, my easily roused optimism stimulated by her gentleness. I remembered that she had been one of the many university students who'd protested and demonstrated against repressive laws.

I helped myself to another drink. Lindy hadn't touched hers.

'I was twenty-one – new here, the son of an English father and an American mother who believed that all human beings should be given an equal opportunity as far as possible . . . Oh, no, what the hell! That has nothing to do with it. I guess I just wanted Veronica . . .'

I began to tell Lindy all about the sad stupid clandestine affair that I had embarked on so lightly and had later so foolishly believed to be a thing of the past. She listened without a single interruption and I knew that she was putting herself in my place – in Veronica's too – trying her best to understand. Knowing Veronica, and having seen the child, helped. At last I put my head into my hands.

'So now, what? Where the devil do we go from here?'

'If you want food I'll get you some —'

'No.'

'Then we'll discuss Veronica's plan.'

'You can't contemplate —'

'Yes,' she said. 'I want that child. Veronica's right. He's worth suffering for. He's clever and . . . beautiful.'

I had a sudden fear that she might want to confide in her mother, but when I voiced it she shook her head.

'No one must guess anything. You're in danger, Derek. The only advice we can take is from John who knows most of this already.'

We talked far into the night. When we went to bed the north-wester had begun to blow and the bare winter branches of the great oak outside our window were lashing themselves into a fury. Rain was in the air. She put a hot water bottle into our big bed to warm her side of it. I had not touched her all evening, but when we drew the blankets up over our shoulders she must have felt me shiver, for she moved close against me and into the hollow of my arm. Her short silky hair was under my lips, her hand was on my chest. She was crying a little now, but I had not lost her. She was still my wife and my lover in spite of everything. I had feared that she would turn away from me but that night she was mine in a different closer way than ever before. That night there was no longer a secret and a deception between us. We were utterly and absolutely one. I had never loved her more.

Lindy felt an affinity with the child straight away and it didn't take her long to make up her mind. But I was worried sick.

John Burford didn't like it either. He visited Veronica and her father and tried to make them see all the dangers of the plan. They saw them all right but they had weighed the pros against the cons and were convinced that the boy must be given the opportunity of going to the top in the privileged white world. What they thought of as 'the top' I have no idea. Prime Minister perhaps! Just as the bootblack in America has the right to dream of becoming President.

In fact, we had no option. Veronica was prepared to go to any lengths to get Lex classified white, even to betraying our relationship as a last resort and paying the penalty for it and having me pay it too. Prison.

So it was finally settled her way.

Once more John acted for me – though he did so reluctantly.

'I don't like seeing Lindy sucked into this thing one hundred per cent,' he said. 'I wish to God I'd never had anything to do with it.'

'We have no choice,' said Lindy.

'I agree,' snapped John. 'Short of breaking up your marriage, you're stuck with Lex. And now what lies do you propose to tell to account for the adoption?'

'We've thought about that,' said Lindy. 'Lex looks like Derek. We must take that into consideration. Derek must have a cousin in England killed in an aircrash. The boy is orphaned and we take him. It's obvious.'

'So simple! Derek's already invented and assassinated an aged aunt, so why not a cousin? But who'll help you put through the adoption?'

'My father's old friend, Canon Carlton, will, I feel sure,' I said. 'If I come clean and tell him everything, he'll understand. He's always been like a second father to me. He has a parish in South Kensington. I'll go straight to him for help. He's a good man.'

'And when the stage is set you'll send for Veronica and Lex?'

'Yes. I'll leave the money for their air passage with you.'

'So I dispatch the time-bomb. Fine! And, let me warn you, time-bomb it is. Fate'll set the clock. You may be sure of that.'

Somehow John's opposition only strengthened our determination. I resented our dependence on his help yet I was grateful for it. He was the only person in the world we could trust. He was linked with us in a peculiar, intimate way and I believe he would have given a great deal at that point to have broken the link and washed his hands of us, but his loyalty to Lindy – and perhaps to me – wouldn't allow him to leave us in the lurch. When he saw us off on the day we sailed it was understood that he would arrange for Veronica to take the next step when we gave the word.

When we arrived in London we found that Canon and Mrs Carlton had already ear-marked a likely home for us – a furnished mews cottage quite near the Rectory. It was just what we wanted.

In a way that cobbled mews in South Kensington had an atmosphere in common with our own lane in the Cape Peninsula. Here too humble stables and cottages had been cleverly converted for more sophisti-cated occupation. When Mrs Carlton showed Lindy over the house she fell in love with it at once. It was built over two garages one of which had been turned into an attractive living-room with an American kitchen-cum-dining-room at the back. Above was a double bedroom for Lindy and me, a tiny study and a little room that would do for Lex. Skylights, that later proved to be rather leaky, made the place light and sunny. The last tenant had used our bedroom as a studio. Under our large living-room window, which was barred as it was at ground level, was a pocket handkerchief garden and we had window-boxes upstairs with geraniums and forget-me-nots. The house was painted lavender with a primrose yellow door which Lindy liked and I found slightly nauseous. However, my whole outlook was jaundiced just then and I dare say the door symbolized it for me.

I felt we'd been bulldozed into a false position and my good sense resisted the positive parenthood Veronica was forcing upon us both. It was extraordinary that Lindy took her part.

'In her place I'd do exactly the same. She doesn't want to be rid of Lex. She adores him. She's putting his interests before everything else in life.'

Lindy and the Carltons clicked at once. The old couple – at least they seemed old to us – were about the same age as her parents – in the fifties – and they had the same endearing simplicity.

'But they have no prejudices,' marvelled Lindy. 'To them all human beings are God's children and that's that. No distinctions. Let's go and see them together and tell them our story.'

So the four of us sat down in their comfortable Victorian study and I told them the whole wretched tale quite frankly, making no excuses.

I think their profound hatred of apartheid and all its ramifications influenced their attitude for they accepted the situation with grave attention and concern and neither of them uttered one word condemning my behaviour which had led to such drastic complications.

'You're doing all you can to make amends, my boy,' said Canon Carlton, his vivid blue eyes more sympathetic than critical. 'And Lindy is showing a true Christian spirit in wanting to accept the great responsibility of your son.'

'I loved Lex the moment I saw him,' said my wife. 'He's a fine little fellow. And we have no children of our own.'

Mrs Carlton bowed her head with its unfashionable grey hair and I saw her furtively touch her eyes with her handkerchief.

'Nor have we,' she said, in a low voice. 'I often wish we'd adopted children, but Sydney insists that his flock is all we need.' She smiled mistily and turned to me. 'Of course we can help you make the adoption arrangements and when you send for the child and his mother they can stay here with us while the formalities are completed. There's a nursery school just round the corner where Lex can go. I'll see the Principal.'

Before the month was out we had moved into our new home and written to John Burford that the time had come to send Veronica and Lex to London.

# 9

## LINDY

*'He's a child of the streets'*

Veronica was only in England for three weeks, the
time it took to complete the adoption formalities. Just
in case there should be any hitches she left her power of
attorney with Canon Carlton.

The Carltons were as good as their word and put up
Veronica and Lex. They agreed with us that the
sooner the break was made the better.

'But see as much of the child and his mother as you
can while she's here, Lindy,' Mrs Carlton advised me.
'He must have confidence in you when he's left in your
care. And let him get used to the mews. He'll enjoy the
come and go of cars – you know how little boys are
about cars – and he's mad on the TV. He's never seen
one before. The more things he likes about you and
your home the easier the break will be.'

Derek went to his office in Blackfriars by tube every
day which left me the use of the little car we had
recently acquired. Lex loved being taken out in it.
Veronica, he and I went to all London's lovely parks

and bathed in the Serpentine. I gave Lex inflatable rubber cuffs that he wore on his arms so that he could make believe he was swimming. He was quite fearless. Derek gave him a boat to sail in the Round Pond and it amused me to watch his uninhibited friendliness with strangers. Most of all he loved the waterfowl in St James's Park – the decorative ducks and the pelicans. We took him in the Underground and on the tops of buses and to him every excursion was a new exciting adventure. Once or twice I took him out alone and he held my hand and hardly seemed to miss Veronica. I remembered that she was accustomed to leaving him all day at the crêche when she went to sew for her ladies at their houses, and that the whole way of his life had encouraged his natural gregariousness.

I asked Veronica about his habits and his likes and dislikes where food was concerned.

'And what time do you put him to bed?'

'Any time,' she said easily. 'In summer when it's hot he stays up till it gets cooler. He's used to playing with the other children round our place for as long as the light lasts.'

'He can't do that here. With daylight saving he could be up till near eleven at night!'

She laughed and shrugged. That would be my problem.

The time came when we moved his pathetic little possessions from the Rectory to the mews. Veronica was to leave early next morning. Dear Mrs Carlton had arranged to drive her to London Airport.

'I'll see her off,' she said. 'It'll be very hard for her – this parting.'

'Do you think she'll go through with it?' I asked.

'Very much so. She's adamant. There's something else, Lindy. She's decided that later on – when the time seems ripe – you must tell Lex she is . . . dead.'

'Dead? I can't!'

'I think perhaps you must. It's the only way to make him completely yours – to allow him to forget her and not feel abandoned.'

'But he probably doesn't know anything about death. He's only a baby!'

'He's rising four. And the children of the poor areas – on the fringes of slums – learn about death at an early age. I've discussed this with Veronica. Lex believes in heaven. Death is natural to him and heaven a lovely dream.'

It was clear that Mrs Carlton and Veronica had established a very close understanding. So, when Veronica attacked me on the subject in her vehement way, I gave in.

'But I don't like it.'

'It's necessary,' she insisted. 'Or he'll keep wondering why I don't fetch him back. He'll feel I've deserted him – however happy you make him. It must be possible for him to think of you as his mother – to call you Mommy. He must never see my father or me or our home again. He must forget that world completely. He *must*!'

I promised that when the opportunity came I'd take it.

'He'll suffer and get over it. That way a clean break can be made,' she said, keeping herself under iron control.

There was no part of this deception – this whole business – that she hadn't considered and allowed for, even if it meant twisting the knife in her heart.

Meanwhile we had told Lex that his mother must return to Cape Town as his oupa was sick, and that he would be staying on in London with us and be our little boy for a while. He had been startled and tearful at first and then had seemed to forget about his mother's imminent departure. But when she brought him to us on her last night and Lex saw her unpack his little suitcase he began to cry in earnest, tears streaming down his cheeks, nose running.

Veronica said in a choked voice, 'This lovely little room – your very own.'

'I don't want to stay here without you.' He sobbed and clung to her.

For the first time I heard him talk in Afrikaans.

He had never slept alone, never been a night away from his mother. I had put a big Teddy bear on his pillow to keep him company, but nothing could comfort him. Mrs Carlton had foreseen this situation and given Veronica a sleeping powder to dissolve in milk. Now she handed it to me, her eyes brimming and desperate.

'In warm milk,' she said. 'Please.'

I left her with the child while I heated the milk and stirred the powder into it. When I went back he was in bed and Veronica was lying beside him.

'I'll stay till he drops off,' she murmured.

She had closed the curtains but even so there was enough light for me to see her face – pinched and ghastly. She sat up and held him against her and he struggled to drink the milk obediently, gulping, sniffing, tears dropping into the glass.

'All of it – to please me,' she begged.

I took the empty glass from her and she sank back again with the child's head on her breast, her arm about him.

When she came downstairs half an hour later her eyes were swollen and bruised. It must have taken all her resolution to stick to her purpose.

'It's not too late,' Derek said gently. 'We can still call the whole thing off.'

She shook her head silently.

'I'll walk back to the Rectory with you,' he said. 'And I'm sure Mrs Carlton will give you one of those powders you gave Lex.'

'Try not to worry about him,' I said. 'I couldn't love him more if he was my own.'

She wanted to say something but failed and shook her head. I saw her go away with Derek, their footsteps uneven on the cobbles.

I went upstairs and looked into the little room where Lex lay in a deep drugged sleep. The Teddy bear was beside him, and, as I touched it, the soft velvety fur was wet.

For Veronica the farewell to her son must have been a sort of death.

When I wrote to my parents about 'the tragedy' of Derek's cousin and his wife being killed in an aircrash and our decision to adopt their only child they accepted the story without question. Perhaps they were rather gullible, but they knew that it was a bitter disappointment to me that Derek and I had not had babies of our own and so I expect they felt that it was only natural we should take 'the orphan' into our home. We had arranged with Veronica that she should tell the truth among her own people and say her son had been adopted by an English family and that she had relinquished all claim to him. Only the identity of the family must remain secret.

At first our poor little boy was subdued and lost and the Teddy bear was damp with tears for several nights, but quite quickly his gay adaptable temperament tided him over the anguish of parting and he perked up and became part of our lives and of the mews and of the nursery school which had reopened for the autumn term. So many things entertained and pleased him. Lex, I discovered, had an infinite capacity for delight. He was enraptured by the red sports car with the long strapped-on bonnet. It belonged to Bill Fairlea, the young bachelor who lived opposite us. Bill's windows were usually open except in the heart of winter and his record player blared out the top of the pops the moment he got home and had stabled his scarlet steed. Lex liked any sort of music and most noises. He loved the zoom and whine of the jets going over South Kensington on their way to London Airport, he revelled in the racy cars that roared in and out of the mews, he rejoiced in the jabber of other people's radios and TVs, in the barking of the next door sausage dog, the miaowing of the black cat, the billing and cooing of the pigeons and the less frequent mewing of gulls seeking crusts in winter.

There were other children in the mews and he was soon accepted as one of their group, though he was younger than most of them.

Veronica and her father had done their utmost to bring him up according to the best European standards. He was reasonably obedient and house-trained though at first we had some difficulty in persuading him that our garden and the mews were not to be piddled in whenever he felt so inclined. Although Afrikaans had been the language of the crêche and of most of his former friends, both Luther Arendse and Veronica had made a habit of talking to him in English and avoiding the *taal* – the mélange of both languages that characterizes coloured conversation. Under our influence, the Afrikaans words soon disappeared from his ever-increasing English vocabulary. At our wish he called us Daddy and Mommy willingly enough and after six months, when he was securely and happily settled with us, we told him that his own mother and oupa had gone to heaven but that he was now our little boy for keeps and we couldn't do without him. Many new impressions had overlaid his misty childish memories of Cape Town and even of Veronica and his grandfather, and after the first questions and a few tears he accepted the new life and relationships with surprising speed and cheerfulness. That was his gift, I thought, the buoyant adaptability he had inherited from Derek.

But, for all that, his early experiences had left their mark. The manners and expressions of the mean streets were not entirely forgotten. So, when Derek came home one evening, he found me in a mood that was both thoughtful and amused. He kissed me and held me away from him, his eyes on my face merry and questioning.

'Lex? What's he been up to now?'

We sat on the wooden bench in our tiny patch of

garden watching our son who was playing with the small boy from two doors down. They were bowling hoops along the cobbles. The sun in his hair was as bright as the early autumn leaves nodding over the church wall. Lex was strong for his age though slightly built.

'Isn't that rather dangerous – playing out there?' Derek asked. 'Even in a cul-de-sac like this.'

'Not for Lex. By instinct and habit he's a child of the streets. He has the traffic sense and quickness of an urchin. The other children in the district where he used to live had no gardens. The street was their playground.'

'It's extraordinary,' he said. 'The way you project yourself into that child's background and mentality.'

I laughed. 'It's not always easy.'

Derek raised one eyebrow. 'For instance?'

'This afternoon, when I fetched him home from school, Miss Adamson asked me to wait and have a word with her.'

'What's he been up to now?'

'Well, I waited for the mums to collect their little darlings and among them was a Jamaican boy – soot black, pure Negro in appearance – and a dark-skinned very pretty little Pakistani girl with long black hair. Her mother wore a sari and was quite gorgeous in her own way. The rest of the children were humdrum little English boys and girls. I noticed that Lex was scowling at the Jamaican child with that sullen smouldering look he puts on when he's in a bad mood. Miss Adamson wasn't missing a trick. There were two chairs on the dais and she offered me one. Lex stood next to me. I had my arm round his shoulders. He was tense as a dog spoiling for a fight.'

'He's relaxed enough now,' Derek pointed at the hoop-bowlers who were shrieking with laughter and excitement.

'Oh yes, he gets over things quickly. Anyway, Miss Adamson explained that Pedro, the Jamaican – he's older and bigger than Lex – sits in front of Lex in class and Aza, the Pakistani girl, sits in front of Pedro. Suddenly, while Miss Adamson was drawing a picture on the blackboard, she heard a squeal and a bellowing and looked round to see Lex hammering Pedro over his woolly head with his fists and worst of all he was shouting at the top of his voice, "Bloody nigger! Bloody nigger!" Miss Adamson said that actually Lex had said "*blerry* nigger" but his meaning was perfectly clear even if the word was slightly mangled.'

'Good God! But why?'

'Aza was crying but Miss Adamson was so busy preventing a fight between Pedro and Lex that she didn't get around to sorting out what started it. She told me she'd punished Lex by making him stand in the corner with his face to the wall. It wasn't for long because it was just on playtime. About five minutes.

Then, when the others had gone into the playground, she gave him a lecture about calling people names and pummelling their heads, but he just turned s ulky and wouldn't say he was sorry. However, she let him go when he said he wanted to go to the loo, but he didn't go any such place. He galloped into the garden, found Pedro and the next thing Miss Adamson saw was Lex spitting at Pedro – "and he can spit a very long way, Mrs Symes", she said – and he was yelling "Do it again, and I'll cut you in little pieces!" '

'Good old coloured threat! But what did he mean by "Do it again –"?'

'That's exactly what I asked her. She was puzzled too, so I asked Lex but he just buried his face against my lap. Then I had an inspiration. I asked him in Afrikaans. "It's our secret language," I whispered to him. "She doesn't understand. You can tell me." And he came clean. "Pedro pulled Aza's hair," he said. "He hurt her so I hurt him." '

Derek threw back his head and laughed and so did I. The pigeons flew down over the mews with a whirr of wings and the sausage dog yapped.

'I hope you translated for Miss Adamson. After all, Lex had provocation and a sense of chivalry.'

'I did. But the trouble wasn't so much the quarrel as Lex's calling Pedro a "blerry nigger". That really flicked Miss Adamson on the raw. She gave me an earful. She said "You come from South Africa, Mrs

Symes, where there is great racial conflict. We object to that here. If Lex uses that expression again in this school he'll be asked to leave. And I'd be very sorry to lose him because he's a cheerful little fellow and highly intelligent." '

'Expelled for obscene language at the age of four and a half! Arrogant little devil. I s'pose it's how his District Six chums talked of the Africans. So, my sweet Lindy, you had to eat humble pie for both of you?'

'Yes – and give Lex a scolding. You'll have to go over the ground with him again tonight. He's quite old enough to know what's naughty. And that swearing and calling people insulting names is very naughty indeed.'

So Derek tackled Lex after I'd put him to bed and heard his prayers. When he came down I said 'Well, how did it go?'

We were in the kitchen and I was stirring a stew. The table was set for our dinner. Derek sat down at it and pressed his fingers hard against the tops of his eye-sockets. His elbows were on the table and he looked dejected.

'I couldn't scold him for taking up cudgels for Aza, but I said it was very naughty to swear at Pedro. I said, "It's not his fault he's black and anyway blacks are just as good as whites." '

'So?'

'So he gave me one of his long mournful reproachful

looks and said, "They aren't – everybody knows they aren't." '

I had to laugh. 'Did you make him understand?'

But Derek wasn't laughing. 'He understands a hell of a lot more than we do, darling – a whole goddamn world that's foreign to us. What's more he remembers.'

He came and put his arms round me as I stood there at the stove and he said,

'We must look out, Lindy. We've taken this child too late.'

# 10

# ANN SEYMOUR

---

*'The hum of the machine was quiet'*

Really, the coloureds fascinate me. I was brought up on a Constantia wine farm and I've known them ever since I drew my first breath. Yet they never cease to astonish me with their extraordinary inconsistencies. Liars, thieves, drunks, moody as hell, kind, loyal, sympathetic, good company, humorous, and a solid class of them, like Veronica Arendse's family, are sterling worth, a God-fearing middle class struggling for a place in the sun. Gifted too – they have their writers, artists, dancers and singers. What singers! Music and rhythm are in their blood, from the coons to the operatic stars in the Eoan Group. And their scholars who must go to non-European libraries to get out their books. What a tragi-farce it is – this petty apartheid! And now for the inconsistency.

Veronica was here sewing for me and it just chanced that I had Kate van Vuuren to tea. We had tea in the patio under the wistaria trellis. The springtime scent of the flowers was intoxicating. I adore wistaria. The room where Veronica sews looks on to the patio and when she wasn't using her machine she could hear every word we said. Funny, but she seemed very busy with her handwork during that hour! The hum of the machine was quiet.

It's over a year now since Lindy and Derek went to London and of course I like to hear news of them.

'I always wonder,' I said, 'why your Lindy adopted a toddler instead of a tiny baby – he'd be nearly five now, wouldn't he? It's so much trickier than an infant with no recollections to counteract.'

'It was chance not choice.' Kate van Vuuren took one of Lizzie's featherlight scones and made short work of it. 'This distant cousin of Derek's was killed with his wife in an air disaster. The child was orphaned and needed a home. If you must adopt – and I think it was far too soon to do anything so drastic but you know how Lindy is – it had better be a relation. Then at least you know what blood you're getting.'

'Derek's family must have a hoodoo on them. His mother and father lost their lives in a car crash, I believe.'

Kate frowned and shivered.

'The coincidence hadn't occurred to me, but it's nasty when you think of it. They must be – what do you call it? – disaster prone.'

'Oh, I shouldn't let it worry you. We all have to take our bow some time or another and I'd rather take mine suddenly than fade away in some dreary illness. But don't let's think morbid thoughts on such a lovely spring day. Tell me about this little grandson.'

'He sounds a fine little chap – great company for Lindy. She writes about him so enthusiastically. I'm dying to see him. As a matter of fact, I have some colour snaps of them here. I'll show you in a minute, but first I must devour another of these delicious scones. I shouldn't, of course, I'm putting on weight.'

She is, come to that, but then that's her Afrikaner blood coming out. The young ones, like Lindy, can be ravishing – all pink and gold and little waists and firm curves – but they end up bulky if they don't watch it. However, there's always something peculiarly satisfying in watching a fattish woman eat more than's good for her – if it's one's own food she's eating – because you appreciate that she's acting against her own interests and deliberately indulging herself which is a compliment to your cook. Kate refused the home-made plum jam and the blob of whipped cream that really makes the scones sublime, and after Lizzie had waddled out to fetch the tea-tray, she fished in her bag for the snapshots.

'This is Lex in the tiny garden of the mews cottage with a neighbour's dog. Rather sweet, don't you think?'

Usually one has to rave when there's nothing to rave about, but this time that wasn't the case. The boy was truly beautiful. I held the little picture in the sun to see it better.

'He's heaven,' I said honestly. 'And the fantastic thing is that he's got a terrific look of Derek. That copper hair and that rather special nostril, very nicely carved. The close-fitting ears and what a pair of eyes!'

Child and daschund were looking straight into the camera.

'Two intelligent faces,' laughed Kate, evidently pleased. 'And here's one of Lex with a girl-friend.'

It was then that Veronica came out on to the patio to ask me if I could spare five minutes to fit a skirt. 'Just for the length,' she said. 'I'm sorry to interrupt.'

'That's all right,' I said, and turned to Kate. 'This is Veronica Arendse who does a bit of sewing for me. As a matter of fact she worked for Lindy before they left for England.'

Kate smiled at the girl.

'I remember. You made my daughter some pretty cottons for the voyage.'

'I was glad to work for Mrs Symes,' said Veronica politely. 'How is she?'

'Very well. She and her husband have adopted a boy – about a year ago. I'm just showing Mrs Seymour some snaps of him.'

'May I see them?'

'Naturally.'

Kate passed Veronica the snapshot of the child and

the dog. She went into the sun and looked at it, her back to us. She looked for a long time and when she turned round her face was that curious ashen colour they go when they aren't well, but she mustered a sort of smile as she gave the picture back to Kate.

'He's a lovely boy,' she said. 'Mrs Symes must be happy.'

'Oh, she is. And there's one here of him with a girlfriend. Have you finished with that snap, Ann?'

I handed it to Veronica. It was a picture of the little boy standing next to a very pretty Indian child with long black hair streaming over her shoulders. They were hand in hand. Evidently outside their school.

Veronica stared at it in disbelief, her eyes narrow and shiny. She gave it back with a gesture of annoyance.

'What is Lex doing with an Indian child?'

Kate shot her a glance of sheer amazement.

'There's no apartheid in England,' she said patiently. 'The children are schoolmates. As a matter of fact, that little girl is the daughter of a very clever Pakistani doctor. He's on the staff of a big London hospital. My daughter and her husband see a lot of the family.'

Veronica did not even deign to reply. Her disapproval was evident in every rigid line of her body. There you have it, the total inconsistency! You'd have expected her, of all people, to applaud such a friendship.

Kate, bewildered, shrugged and put the snaps back

in her bag. I rose quickly and said, 'Let's get that fitting done, Veronica. It won't take five minutes, Kate. I'll be right back.'

While she was pinning up the hem, I said, 'Veronica, how did you know that child's name was Lex?'

I guessed she'd been eavesdropping. They always do. They are perpetually convinced that we have nothing better to do than talk about them. I suppose, in a way, it's true. When two women get together the subject of servants invariably crops up. Thank heaven we still have them in this country! We all know the personalities of our friends' servants as they, no doubt, know ours. And then the Government thinks it can prevent integration! We couldn't be more closely integrated than we are, even if it is on an employer-employee basis.

Veronica took some pins from between her lips before she answered me.

'I couldn't help hearing you and Mrs van Vuuren talk. The window is open and I was interested because I like Mrs Symes. Mrs van Vuuren mentioned the adopted boy, Lex.'

'You didn't like the picture of him with the Pakistani girl.'

'I don't like Indians.'

'You don't like apartheid. In London they try not to have any. You should approve of that.'

She made no reply.

'There,' she said, kneeling back on her heels. 'That seems right to me. Do you find it too short, Mrs Seymour?'

The subject of Lex and apartheid was dismissed. When they know they're being unreasonable they go into a sulk. They can be infuriating but somehow, if you really understand them, you can't help liking them.

But it's queer how the incident stuck in my mind. Why had the girl cared so passionately what friendship a little boy – quite unknown to her – might have formed far away in London? I suppose it's all rooted in this everlasting racial strife and consciousness we live with here. The coloureds regard the Africans as 'bloody niggers' and they fear the financial genius of the Indians who so often own the houses the coloureds live in. Somehow the Indians prosper and rise above their beginnings and become shopkeepers, financiers or professional men – men to be reckoned with. They, like the Malays, have the heritage of a culture more ancient than our own. Of a caste system too, more rigorous and deep-seated than our stupid apartheid, which will one day go with the wind.

I took Veronica home to District Six. Her father has quite a nice villa there up on the slope of Devil's Peak. He was sitting on his stoep with a studious-looking Indian when I stopped outside the gate. They were deep in conversation. So he, at least, didn't object to Indians!

'Haven't you a little boy?' I asked Veronica as she got out of the car. I remembered Hope van der Spuy telling me about the fair-skinned child she had seen playing in the little garden.

'No, Mrs Seymour,' she said brusquely. 'I have no little boy.'

I saw the Indian rise to meet her, and her father take his pipe out of his mouth and push his glasses up on to his forehead. Hope says he's really very nice. He has a rather aesthetic face.

The sinking sun fell in a long amber shaft between Lion's Head and Table Mountain. It funnelled over the upper city of Cape Town and petered out in the crowded streets of District Six.

I drove past the schoolhouse destined to be for whites only in future and back on to the de Waal Drive. I turned south between the bay and the pine forests around Hospital Bend towards the southern suburbs and the leafy homes of the privileged. But Veronica lingered in my mind. She had behaved very curiously with Mrs van Vuuren. There was something volcanic about that girl.

# 11

# JOHN BURFORD

---

*'Derek's afraid of Lex's memory'*

Feeling as I do about Lindy, it was playing with fire to take my Christmas holiday in London, but, by then, I was so deeply involved with Derek and Lindy and Lex that I made no real attempt to resist my impulse to pay them a flying visit. After all, it was eighteen months since I had seen them and I was all burnt up with curiosity and misgivings about the whole business. I absolutely had to know how it was shaping. Or maybe that was just the excuse I gave myself for wanting to see Lindy.

I arrived the day before Christmas Eve. The plane was late and it was noon when we touched down, a cold sunless day with a north wind blowing that cut into one's bone marrow, or so it seemed to me coming straight from the height of the hot South African summer. Lindy and Lex were there to meet me and I gave them lunch at the airport.

Lindy was wearing a fur coat and a fur cap a couple of shades darker than her hair. The cold and the wind

130

had whipped colour into her cheeks, her eyes were a deeper blue than I had remembered, more lapis lazuli than blue agate – or it could be that they reflected this sombre English sky differently – and she had grown from a pretty girl into a lovely woman. She had the same ready spontaneous smile but there was a new dimension in her expression which I found hard to interpret. Wisdom and a trace of disillusion? She had never held any mystery for me in the bright atmosphere of our own country, yet here, in the furs that made her look Scandinavian, frosty as the Polar star, I was face to face with an intriguing foreigner.

The little boy who scampered and pranced beside her was snugly dressed in long corduroy trousers and a quilt-ed yellow anorak. His crisp not too wavy hair was russet and his dancing eyes were black as night. The likeness to Derek was – apart from those brilliant sad-happy eyes – disturbing.

'He's been so excited watching the planes come and go,' she said. 'It's the most thrilling day of his life.'

'Daddy's gone to work,' he announced. 'So Mommy brought me to meet you. I'm having Christmas holidays.'

I felt her glance at me, half amused, half inquisitive, to see how I would take the Daddy-Mommy touch. I raised one eyebrow and grinned and suddenly she laughed.

'Old cynic! You didn't believe it possible, did you?'

'Frankly, I don't know what I believed. Nothing would surprise me any more.'

They'd fixed me up with a divan in Derek's study and there was a cupboard on the landing Lindy had cleared for me.

'Not the height of luxury and you've got to put up with my cooking. But we didn't think you'd mind for a fortnight.'

I had never known Lindy go near her stove at home. She left all that to Minnie. Here she bathed Lex, gave him his supper, put him to bed and cooked a simple but excellent meal for Derek, herself and me. While we were sitting over our coffee, which we had in the living-room downstairs, Lex, sleepless and over-excited, wandered in wearing a tartan dressing-gown over his sleeping suit. No one scolded him or sent him packing and he crept on to his father's knee and curled up like a puppy. When he fell asleep Derek carried him up to bed and tucked him up.

'That was one of the difficult things,' said Lindy. 'He wasn't used to regular bedtime hours. In the old days, before he came to us, I s'pose he used to play about till it was dark or he was sleepy. When we took him – when we first arrived here – it was still daylight saving and to get him to sleep before ten or eleven was real hard work. He used to cry at night. Not any more.'

I recalled the bedroom in the house in District Six where I had first seen Lex, a baby asleep in a basket on his mother's bed. I guessed that he had shared Veronica's bed and having a room of his own had been a sort of weaning. Painful probably for both of them.

'What does he think has happened to Veronica?' I asked.

'He thinks she's dead,' said Lindy. 'That was the way she wanted it.'

Lindy talked about Lex a good deal and it was clear that he was company for her and that she seldom gave an unnecessary thought to his origin. She had eliminated all sentiment on the subject and studied her son objectively, taking his early environment into consideration only when she believed that it influenced his present behaviour. At university she had studied psychology and social science and she was capable of applying her theoretical knowledge to the day-to-day facts of her life with Lex. But I wondered if she really understood Derek's profound inner resentment to the lifelong responsibility which his casual acts of self-indulgence had incurred. I suspect he sometimes looked at the ivory and rosy face of his son and wished that it could have been brown, in which case that would have been that! But, superficially, he certainly made the best of things. His was a kind and volatile nature and the child was happy and at home with him. All the same I felt that by imposing Lex upon the marriage Veronica might have driven a wedge between Derek and Lindy. Not that she'd care so long as Lex profited.

On Christmas day, when the first church bells pealed, it was snowing. I had forgotten the beauty of gently whirling snowflakes and of white rooftops. The mews cobbles were lightly blanketed and sound was muted except for the chiming insistent bells.

Lindy and Derek called me into their bedroom to wish me happy Christmas and we exchanged presents. Lex was sitting up in bed between them emptying a large red net stocking over the eiderdown. It was a cornucopia of toys. Among them was a black lamb. Lex showed it to me.

'This is for Baby Jesus,' he announced.

Then he forgot it as I gave him a miniature aeroplane that could actually fly. It was a huge success.

Later we went to the Children's Service, crunching through the snow and across the church gardens where the trees were transfigured by the white frosty magic of that cold quiet windless morning. Lex clutched the black lamb in his little gloved hand.

The church looked festive and to the right of the entrance was a splendid Christmas tree and beneath it the crib with Mary holding her Babe in swaddling clothes on her lap with Joseph suitably in the background as he always was, poor fellow, and the three Kings paying homage. There was the manger and a cow and a donkey and some hens and chickens, a dog and cat and a shepherd with some white sheep. Lex bent over the crib and confidently placed his black lamb in it in a place of honour near the Holy Infant.

Afterwards I asked Lindy why he had felt it necessary to add his personal contribution to the traditional scene. She puckered her eyebrows.

'I don't really know. Last year – his first Christmas with us – he was very upset when he saw the crib and there was no black sheep. I had to go out and buy him one as soon as the shops re-opened, and he added it. This year I took no chances. He insists that Jesus always has a black lamb and loves it most of all his flock.'

'I can account for that. In the front room of the Arendse house there's a big picture of the Good Shepherd carrying a crook and a black lamb.'

'I see,' she said thoughtfully. 'He must have quite a retentive memory.'

That afternoon the snow stopped falling and the early winter dark was freezing cold. Derek drove us to Trafalgar Square to see the giant Christmas tree and all the lights of theatreland and the West End. Lex was madly excited.

'It's Fairyland!' he kept crying out. 'I know it's Fairyland!'

I suspected that he remembered the other 'Fairyland' which had so often delighted him and Veronica.

He went to bed that night with his new toys all round him and Lindy said, 'What are you going to dream about?'

'Baby Jesus and the lamb and Fairyland.'

'Nice,' she said, and kissed him and tucked him in.

He was tired and fell asleep at once which was just as well as Lindy and Derek had friends to share the turkey – Bill Fairlea, the young artist from across the mews, and his girl-friend, a girl for me, who was jolly and wholesome and very English and not a patch on Lindy, and a Pakistani doctor, Hyat Khan, and his wife, Gulab, whose little daughter was evidently a great pal of Lex's. The wife, whose name means Rose in her own language, is a beauty and they are both very pleasant and sophisticated, and, although they are Muslims, they enjoyed a glass of champagne.

'It's the sort of friendship one could never form at home,' said Lindy after they had gone. 'But one day it will be possible. The fantasy of total apartheid can't last for ever.'

Derek grinned, his teeth flashing and his eyes full of laughter.

'You'd better not talk that way to your parents when you get home.'

'My parents belong to the die-hard generation. But they know we've got Pakistani friends here and they don't object, or, if they do, they haven't said so in their letters.'

'That's how it goes with most sensible South Africans,' said Derek. 'When you're abroad you behave differently. You throw off your racial shackles to a great extent. But when you go back to South Africa it's back to the pigeon-holes and the rules. Nothing short of a goddamn revolution will ever change that.'

'No one can foresee the end of the chapter in our country,' I said rather irritably. 'But personally I believe there'll be a modified change of heart. When we're hemmed in by the developing independent Bantu states the whites and the coloureds will join forces as a matter of expediency and there'll be a much smaller, much more integrated and tolerant South Africa than exists at present.'

'Oh, God,' groaned Derek. 'Not politics on Christmas night! Let's pray for peace and goodwill in the world —'

'And dream of Fairyland like Lex,' added Lindy.

'Mmm . . .' I gave her an old-fashioned look, kissed her good-night under the mistletoe and marvelled that a spoilt South African girl could turn out a slap-up Christmas dinner alone and unaided.

Derek was not on holiday, so during the next ten days I saw more of Lindy than I had done since he had appeared on the scene some five years ago. We took Lex to Kensington Gardens to sail his toy boats when the weather was reasonable. We took him to pantomimes and children's shows at various cinemas and sometimes the little Pakistani girl, Aza, came with us. One afternoon Lex went to a party at Aza's home and we left him there and went back to the mews, having arranged to fetch him later.

'It's good for him to be without me occasionally,' said Lindy.

'I couldn't agree more,' I said with feeling.

She laughed. 'We're not usually in each other's pockets all day. He goes to school. But, like you, he's having holidays.'

She had a coal fire in the living-room.

'It makes more work, but it's so much nicer.'

'I don't know you in this role. Housewife, doing everything. And mother into the bargain.'

'I have a charlady two mornings a week.'

'Not enough.'

'Quite enough when Lex is at school.'

She had made our tea by the fireside and there were hot buttery crumpets. Luscious. She was curled up on the small couch in warm slacks and a chunky sweater. It was the first time we had really been alone together in the cottage. Her fresh unstudied prettiness never failed to move and entrance me. We were cosy and relaxed and I risked a very personal question.

'Do you think – has it ever struck you – that Lex may come between you and Derek? Just a little.'

She considered her answer with that tiny puckering

of her eyebrows that set a shadow between them that would one day be a furrow.

'Is that your impression?' she said, at last.

It was my turn to think.

'It could happen.'

'I know.'

My heart gave a lurch. Lindy is so honest. These two were my best friends, yet the thought of a rift was not unbearable. I was afraid of my own rush of feeling. Suddenly we were very close indeed, linked by the need I had sensed in Lindy to confide in someone. After all, there was no one in the world she could talk to about this particular problem except me. She was utterly alone with it.

'Like to tell me?'

'Why not? You know all of us – Derek, me, the child, even his . . . real mother.'

'Go ahead. Let off steam, Lindy. I guess you must get pretty pent up from time to time.'

Her eyes were wide and concentrated, their deepest blue. 'You know how easy-going and optimistic Derek is by nature – well, sometimes I think that's changing. Usually he can forget anything it doesn't suit him to remember and he has such a talent for enjoyment, such high spirits. He still has. We have tremendous fun together a lot of the time and Lex makes him laugh because he and Derek have the same exuberance. But naturally they clash too and if ever I take Lex's part

Derek resents it. You see, Lex is a living reproach – a reminder of something he'd prefer never to think about again.'

'Well, that's his own look out. And he's very lucky you took up the attitude you did.'

'I'm not so sure about that. He said once that if I'd dug in my toes and refused to have anything to do with it – if I'd threatened to leave him – he could have called Veronica's bluff —'

'It wasn't a bluff. Make no mistake about that! She was acting on a very strong instinct and with a very powerful motive. She wanted her son to be brought up white. It was possible.'

'She banked on my falling for Lex – which I did. I don't regret it – though I see the shoals ahead. He'll grow up and fall in love . . . and then . . . what? Those dark genes —'

'As Veronica said, meet that when it comes.'

'One day it'll be essential to tell Lex the truth, the whole truth and nothing but the truth. When he's an adult, old enough, brave enough and strong enough to face it. Meanwhile can we keep the secret in the Cape Peninsula? We'll never feel quite safe there – as we are here.'

'Veronica has sworn never to lay any claim to him and never to try to see him.'

'People break vows. I think those are the dangers that worry Derek. He's doing very well and he's been offered the top job in Cape Town. It'd be mad not to take it. Anyway, he adores the Cape – as I do, and we go back next July. Mummy and Daddy are thrilled. They miss me.'

'I know they do.'

'How did they really take this adoption? Their letters weren't enthusiastic.'

'Mrs van Vuuren thought the boy was too old, but, as your father pointed out, he was orphaned by a catastrophe and you and Derek were the heaven-sent solution to a very sad problem.'

She smiled, her mouth soft and tender.

'Dear Daddy, bless his good heart!'

She uncoiled her long legs and went across to a little writing-desk where she rummaged in a drawer till she found a child's painting book. She brought it to me and sat on the arm of my chair.

'Mummy sent this to Lex for his birthday. Here's something that might interest you.'

The plain line pictures for children to fill in with paints or crayons were illustrations of classic fairy tales.

'Here's Beauty and the Beast —'

'Lex has a vivid taste for colour,' I remarked.

'Malay,' she laughed, 'or just plain modern? Here's Snow White and the Seven Dwarfs.'

Her nearness was more disturbing than she knew. She turned the page and waited for my reaction. I gave a low whistle.

'So the dwarfs are all brown men. Red and green costumes, brown faces.'

'I asked Lex why. He said "Dwarfs are coloured people." I told him they could be anything.'

'Danie Jacobs, the hunchback.'

She nodded. 'He must remember that man. Derek's afraid of Lex's memory. When he saw this it worried him.'

'I don't suppose it's a definite recollection,' I said. 'It's probably vague – a rough impression of somebody harmless and rather freakish that he can't place.'

I hoped I was right. I didn't much care just then. I was thinking of Lindy on the arm of my chair, her warm breast practically brushing my cheek as she leaned forward to take the painting book from my hands. She said, 'I'll just wash up the tea-things and then we must fetch Lex.'

I helped her dry and a few minutes later we were strolling round to the Khan's flat. The snow had melted, the faint silvery sun had long since gone down, there was frost in the air and a foggy halo surrounded the street lamps as the early winter night set in. Lindy was in her furs, alien, Scandinavian, *la princesse lointaine*.

# 12

# LINDY

*'Going back won't be easy'*

John went back to South Africa. I missed him. I could talk to John about almost anything – even about Derek and Lex and me.

Before he left he said:

'You're going to be all right, Lindy. Everything's going to be all right. No one can help loving Lex. He's naughty and moody sometimes, but who isn't? He's bright and gay, vital, funny and intensely affectionate. If I was worried about you when I came here I'm not any more. You'll soon be a real family. In fact, you are already.'

'A family haunted by the past and by fears for the future?' I wanted to be reassured.

'A family living in the present.'

'I dread going back to the Cape,' I admitted. 'It's the loveliest place on earth but the Peninsula is a snakepit of gossip and speculation. We'll have to brush up the fiction of our son's parents and their tragic demise.'

He grinned. 'You're right.'

'Mummy will put me through a catechism on the subject. She's a darling but she's madly inquisitive and she doesn't mind interfering.'

'Everybody interferes in other people's affairs in a small society.'

'It's been a wonderful experience being on our own here. Making new friends —'

'Some of them fairly exotic.'

I laughed, knowing he had the Hyat Khans in mind. 'And absorbing new ideas and being completely free of criticism and comment. Going back won't be easy.'

'You'll take it in your stride.'

'Perhaps you'll be married by the time we meet again.'

'Anything can happen. But my guess is no.'

He has a mischievous face, but when it's serious it's rather sad. How close sorrow is to the surface of people's eyes – like sea water that can be warm round your heart and icy round your ankles.

'Dear John,' I said. 'Don't leave it too long.'

Yet, if he married, something important would be gone from my life. The faithful friend – a dull role that could become dangerous. A wife would certainly neutralize the danger!

The boisterous English spring came with its gales and fitful sunshine, its blossom and glorious explosion of young leaf on great trees. The velvet countryside glowed green, laced with silver streams, winding lanes and flowering hedgerows. The small paintable villages embodied a nation's history, ancient, feudal, and often bloodthirsty.

Lex liked the fields and the parks, but he was essentially a child of the mews, gaping in constant delight at Bill's red sports car, feeding the pigeons, romping with the Smiths' sausage dog or shrieking with a flock of other kids as gregarious as himself. He did well at his nursery school, and my father wrote that he had put him down to be a boarder at his own old school in the Peninsula but that Lex wouldn't be accepted till he was seven so he could go to a pre-prep school in the meantime. Well done, Daddy! To get into a good school at the Cape is as difficult as it is anywhere else in the world.

Then it was the end of June and time for us to think about packing up the mews cottage.

'I shall hate leaving it,' I said to Derek. 'We've learned to know each other here in a different way . . . I can't quite explain.'

'I can, honey. You've proved yourself – as a woman, a wife, a mother.'

I shook my head, but he grasped me and hugged me and Lex squeezed between us to be included in the hug.

Soon after that I asked Gulab Khan if she could take Lex home with Aza after school on a certain Friday afternoon.

'I have to go to the dentist,' I said. 'And I really couldn't cope with Lex being there.'

She laughed. 'I should say not. He'd be operating the drill before anyone could stop him! Don't bother about him. Just collect him from us when you're through.'

'Did he hurt – did the dentist hurt?' asked Lex when I arrived at the Khan's flat. Aza was close behind him, her little face troubled as she echoed, 'Did he hurt?'

I felt the hot colour flame over my throat and cheeks and a wave of dizziness passed over me and left me weak. I sat down. Gulab had gone to put the kettle on for tea.

'Not really,' I said to the children. 'No, she didn't hurt.'

'She?' Aza's eyes widened. 'I didn't know there were lady dentists.'

'Oh, yes – yes there are.'

'Your hand's cold as ice!' Lex's chubby fingers had curled into my palm. 'It's wet.'

'It's been raining,' I said.

Early in the following week, when Lex was in bed, Derek and I drank our after-dinner coffee in our tiny garden. It was hot as only London can be in the summer, airless, as if too many million people had been breathing too little oxygen. Our cottage border was alight with fox-gloves, peonies, larkspur, columbines and sweet williams in the long tired twilight.

'You look a bit done in,' said Derek. 'You need a holiday.'

'Soon there'll be the voyage home. What better holiday could we have?'

'None, really.'

He picked up the tray and carried it indoors for me. When he came back the next door cat was sitting beside me washing its face with delicate care. He shoved it off the bench and took its place.

'You shouldn't do that! It's a lucky black cat,' I protested.

'It hasn't gone far.'

The cat threw him a look of disdain and settled at my feet in the age-old sphinx position. It began to purr as I touched its head.

'I didn't go to the dentist on Friday, Derek.'

'Why not?'

'I went to Dr Mary Walsh instead.'

'Who's she?'

'A gynaecologist.'

'Oh, Lord, honey, there's nothing wrong, is there?'

His eyes were full of concern as he moved to stare at me. I laughed.

'Not a thing. Everything's wonderfully right! I got the result of the test today. I wouldn't tell you anything before. I was so afraid I might be mistaken.'

'Lindy!'

'Yes. It's true.'

'When?'

'Next March.'

'That's wonderful! After five years I'd begun to think it wasn't on.'

The front door was open and a little figure pattered out in his shortie pyjamas.

'It's too hot to sleep.'

I put out my arms and he came to me. The cat stalked away haughtily. I took Lex on to my lap and held him against me. His eyes were heavy and shiny, his head nodded. I spoke to Derek across the russet hair.

'Dr Walsh said it might have made all the difference having this one. She said we were very wise. It's often the way.'

My husband looked at the child on my lap with new tenderness.

'Darling,' he said. 'I'm so happy – for you, for all of us.'

Dusk had fallen. Lights glowed behind open windows. Bill was playing one of his more soothing records and we could hear his girl-friend laugh. Our few street lamps leapt into life and Derek took the sleeping boy from my arms. I followed him into the house and locked the door behind us.

'I'm longing to tell Mummie – and John,' I said.

But Derek paused at the foot of the stairs.

'Not just yet,' he said. 'Let it be something

we share – just the two of us – for a little while longer.'

I heard the tiny barb of jealousy sharpen his tone and I was glad.

'We'll wait till we get home,' I said. 'It'll be time enough to tell them then.'

# 13

## ANN SEYMOUR

---

*'That dwarf isn't a stranger'*

The young Symes family came back from England with their adopted child early in August.

They arrived on one of those gorgeous days – the end of a gale – and the feel of an early spring just round the corner. The oak leaves were still close furled but the squirrels were active again, chasing each other through the bare branches. The little boy was soon out in the lane watching them. He'd never seen squirrels before. Lindy ran out after him in a panic.

'He's a terror, Ann, he will insist on exploring!' she called out.

I'd been sitting on my stoep and I came down the steps into the lane which was full of dead oak leaves and acorns. It's infuriating the way the street-sweepers overlook us. Our car tyres crunch over dried acorns every time we draw up against the kerb.

'I'll keep an eye on him while you get on with your unpacking.' I turned to the child. 'What's your name, my lad?'

He fixed me with his sparkling black eyes and said, 'Alexander Symes. You can call me Lex.'

'Can I indeed? Well, then, come on to my stoep, Lex, and maybe I can find you a chocolate.'

'You're an angel,' said Lindy. 'He's awfully friendly. When you want to get rid of him just pack him off, but please make him come *home*! He's like a puppy with a tendency to stray.'

She hurried back to the business of settling in and Lex scampered up the steps and into my house. We had no difficulty finding a chocolate. I always keep them for my bridge friends who make beasts of themselves, especially dear Kate van Vuuren who can never resist anything fattening.

'Your grandmother likes these best,' I said, pointing out a peppermint cream. 'But I think you'd prefer something sweet.'

He smiled and looked up at me merrily through a fringe of navy blue lashes. I thought that he really was most engaging, he had magnetism, that indefinable something they call charisma.

'I could try both and tell you,' he suggested.

'You could indeed.'

That was the beginning of a friendship. We had a lot in common. We both preferred watching the life of the lane to the charms of our respective patios. When eventually the coloured street-sweepers came with their horse and cart, their spades and their dazzling yellow plastic coats, Lex was enthralled. It wasn't long before he was gabbling away to them in Afrikaans. I could never have believed any child of six could pick up a foreign language so quickly. It was phenomenal. Lindy explained it by saying he had a remarkable ear for music. I had already discovered that for myself. I have a record-player and one afternoon, when I was playing some of my records, Lex was lured on to the stoep to listen. I found him there.

'Bill had one in the mews,' he said. 'He let me come in when he was playing it. Bill lived opposite us.'

'I'll let you come in too when I'm playing mine. Right now if you like.'

It was Debussy's 'L'Après-midi d'un Faune'. Believe it or not, that child began to dance, improvising steps and pirouettes, his skinny little-boy legs following the rhythm of that magical summer afternoon when the faun frolics in his sylvan glade. He really looked like a faun too, with his close-fitting slightly pointed ears, his coppery hair and the great Bambi eyes with their vast range of expression from animal wariness to gay self-confidence and occasional melancholy. When the music tailed away he curled up and pretended to fall asleep.

Derek used to take him to school on the way to the office and Lindy or one of the other mothers collected him in the afternoons. There are plenty of children in our neighbourhood and soon he had made friends with

them and they all played in each other's gardens. But
I have an idea he'd have preferred the freedom of the
lane.

One hot morning in the New Year Lindy gave me a
lift back home from the shopping-centre. It was quite
a squeeze for her to get behind the wheel of her car
then! She came in for a cool drink and a chat.

'Heavens, I'll be thankful when the next few weeks
are over and the infant and I are two separate entities,'
she gasped. She was always rather out of breath at that
time. 'I'm dying for some new clothes. I never want to
see these again.'

'You must get Veronica to make you a few things,'
I suggested. 'She doesn't go out sewing any more. She
has set up on her own in a room in her father's house
and she has a Malay girl to help her.'

'Oh,' she said. 'I'll think about it.'

'I can give you her address and telephone number.
She's always very booked.'

'Don't trouble,' she put in quickly. 'I can't bother
with anything till after the baby.'

She sounded quite upset, as if everything was suddenly too much for her. Perhaps I felt like that too
before my children were born. I can't say I remember.
I seem to have been an elderly widow with big
grandchildren for ever.

'Tell me,' I said. 'Does Lex know he's adopted?'

She hesitated. 'All that was two and a half years ago.

He knew then, but he was so small, and he came to accept us as his parents. We never refer to anything before he came to us. Nor does he. One day, of course, he'll have to know the facts – but not while he's still a child.'

She looked distressed and I regretted my curiosity.

'He's a splendid child,' I said. 'How's he getting on at school?'

'He's very happy. He loves school and his homework doesn't trouble him. Next year he'll be a boarder. That'll shake him.'

'I shouldn't think so. He's astonishingly friendly —'

'I'm always telling him not to talk to strangers and never to accept lifts,' she broke in. 'His friendliness is quite a menace.'

'I can believe that. You know, only yesterday I noticed him chumming up with a little coloured hunchback—'

'A hunchback!'

She turned pale. It's curious seeing somebody change colour as you watch. Lindy has a very fair skin and the blood underneath it ebbs and flows visibly when she's agitated.

'Don't worry too much,' I said. 'I was keeping an eye on him. I was on my stoep watering my plants and he was out in the lane – on the sidewalk – watching the squirrels playing in the big oak. They fascinate him. Then this little hunchback materialized out of the shadows and stood staring at him. I had half a mind to call Lex but I thought it best to see what happened.'

'What did happen?' The little gasp was in her voice.

'Lex seemed to become aware of him and turned round. As he did so the hunchback said, "Do you remember me?" – "Kan jy my onthou?" – and Lex looked puzzled and ruffled his hair up with the flat of his little hand as he does when he's thinking and then suddenly his face brightened and he said, "Ja, seker" and the hunchback said "So! Who am I?" Lex laughed and hopped up and down as he said, "You're one of Snow White's dwarfs! Take me to Fairyland!" That was when I got worried. I was afraid the dwarf might try to take him away – kidnap him. It was too easy at that moment. But he only grinned and said "One of these days, klein baas. Ag, ja, one of these days I'll take the snow white boy to Fairyland." '

'I hate it!' Lindy cried in absolute terror. 'It frightens me.'

I went on: 'The hunchback touched his cap to Lex in a mocking sort of way – a salute to the little master, the klein baas – and then he mooched away up the lane and round the corner. He has a funny way of walking – cat-like. Then Lex came on to my stoep and I told him very severely that he mustn't talk to strangers.'

'What did he say?'

'Now I come to think of it, he gave me quite an odd answer. He said "That dwarf isn't a stranger. I know him. He's out of a story – but I can't remember the story." '

Lindy was chalk-white by then and I made her lie down and brought her a neat brandy. She pulled herself together.

'It's the baby,' she said. 'I get nervous about all sorts of things. If ever you see Lex with that hunchback again please tell me at once. But call him away first. Don't let him talk to coloured people, Ann! It's important. Such awful things can happen to children —'

She was getting over-excited and breathless again and I soothed her to the best of my ability.

The baby was born in March. A brother for Lex. I gather Lex is jealous. He's been the kingpin for too long. Lindy's fat cook-general, Minnie, told my maid, Lizzie, that she'd heard Lex talking to the baby one afternoon when he thought nobody was near. He was saying, 'You bloody baby! I'll cut you up in little pieces!' Minnie told Lindy and Lindy told Derek and Lex got a spanking. He certainly deserved it, but won't it just add fuel to the fire?

# 14

## DEREK

---

*'Where's this leading?'*

From the day Mark was born Lex showed signs of jealousy. I'm no psychologist and children aren't easy to understand. To Lindy and me it always seemed that Lex was, if anything, too much of an extrovert, and – let's face it – a child of the city and the street by instinct. We often had to remind ourselves that he had spent the first years of his life in a slummy district where children were accustomed to hunting in packs and finding their entertainment in the gutters. In one way he had been unique. He had been an only child all his life, even in that teeming area of big families and swarming hordes of children both inside and outside the home.

They say that everything you experience from the hour of your birth is recorded on your brain, although the record may never be re-played or the scenes actually visualized, and it was a constant source of anxiety to us that Lex's early memories might be stimulated by our return to the Cape. After Mark's birth this anxiety increased as Lex's resentment of his new brother had the effect of driving him out of the house even more than usual. Of course, he was at school during the week and he often played in friends' gardens in the afternoons, but he was reluctant to come home where he would find Lindy occupied with the baby, feeding or bathing him. Sometimes he would watch the two of them with a brooding precocious look in his melting dark eyes that could be so lively one moment and reflect the sorrows of the universe the next. When I saw him then I doubted if he was really so extrovert after all. At times it seemed that his soul dwelt in some sombre shadowy world impossible for us to penetrate. I tried to say as much to Lindy.

'He's night and day. There's a dark introspective side of him we can't reach. The other is pure sunshine.'

'You're thinking of what Minnie told us – the time she heard him threaten the baby. Don't take it too seriously. Remember Pedro, the Jamaican child, at school in London? He never repeated the offence. He won't with Mark. It's just that it's hard for him to play second fiddle. We must see that he doesn't feel left out.'

My heart lifted. If she could take it lightly I could. Normally Lex was merry as a cricket. Mark's arrival had thrown him off balance. It would pass.

Lindy, who'd been nervous and irritable before Mark's birth, had acquired a new understanding and serenity. He was a healthy, easy infant and when she held him in her arms my young wife personified every mother and child statue or picture of classic fame. It was the expression in her eyes, the softening of her lips, the droop of her slender neck as she looked down at the small head as fair as her own, and the protective hands, supple and gentle, holding him to her breast. She beamed love on to her baby, but when Lex appeared the beam widened to include him. Gradually we felt his antagonism weakening. We were well on the way to being a happy family again.

One evening I brought John Burford home to dinner. Lindy had put the children to bed – Lex in his usual room that had once been used as a sewing-room and Mark in my dressing-room – and we were sitting out on the patio with our drinks. The summer had lingered on into April and the evening was soft and fragrant with the scent of late roses in the air. It was still light although it was after seven. Minnie was, as usual, late with dinner. Lindy had long since given up trying to teach her punctuality.

Lindy has a lovely face, it is also pathetically naked. Thoughts and feelings drift across it and, if you know her, you can read them as you can read the direction of the wind from the cloud shadows scudding across the Cape vineyards and ruffling the leaves. But it always gives me a curious stab of surprise, not quite pleasant, to find John picking up the storm signals as he did that evening.

'Anything wrong?' he asked Lindy.

'There's something I don't like,' she said. 'It happened before Mark was born and again today. Ann Seymour told me. That coloured hunchback – he was hanging around here – getting into conversation with Lex.'

I frowned, not liking it either. The time it had happened before had seriously disturbed us both and it was bad news that the hunchback was still interested in Lex.

Before John could answer or I could question Lindy further Lex came pattering out, barefoot and without a dressing-gown.

'I can't sleep,' he said, and climbed on to my knee. He smelt warm and soapy and his head lay against my shoulder. I ducked my chin to touch his hair and it seemed to me that it was less silky, more wiry these days.

John's face, which had shadowed at Lindy's words, cleared as he smiled at Lex and said,

'Hullo, young fellow.'

'Hullo,' said Lex amiably.

'Lex,' I said gently. 'Who is this little coloured man you talk to in the lane?'

'He's a dwarf. He says one night he'll take me to Fairyland. He laughs and says "Snow white boy, we go to Fairyland." '

Lindy drew in her breath sharply.

'Never go anywhere with anyone you don't know, Lex! Never. No matter who.'

'I know him.' The child nestled closer against me and his eyes became two shining drowsy slits. 'He says there's someone in Fairyland wants to see me.'

After dinner, when he was asleep, and we were having our coffee, Lindy said, in something like panic, 'Where's this leading? What goes on?'

'I'll find out,' said John. 'Jacobs was the go-between. I know his address. I'll write and tell him to come and see me in my flat. Frankly I don't fancy this business any more than you do. Why should he molest the child?'

I realized then that I'd made my friend into a go-between too and the old guilt came up in my throat like vomit. John had conducted the payments and kept me out of the whole dreary transaction to the best of his ability. And here he was offering to carry the can once more.

I left it to him.

But before he could take any action something even more disturbing happened. The very next day. It had nothing to do with the hunchback.

# 15

## KATE VAN VUUREN

---

*'Just a sensation of loving'*

I have felt all along that there were some curious
discrepancies and coincidences in the story of Lex's
adoption.

Lindy and I have always been very close. After all,
she is our only child and no doubt Hendrik and I have
spoilt her but in return she has given us her confidence
and in most matters of importance she relied upon our
advice. I must admit, however, that when it came to
marrying Derek we had our doubts. But she made
mincemeat of them. She was stubborn as a mule. John
Burford had wanted to marry her for years and we
knew his background and his people. He's a fine
young fellow doing well in his profession and he
comes from a good Eastern Province family. One day
he'll be very well off. By comparison, what did we
really know about Derek? He was a foreigner and we
hadn't met his parents. For the matter of that, they
were dead (so he had a small private income) and there
was an old aunt to whom he made an allowance, but

the whole background picture was hazy. His father had been English and his mother American. Politically he didn't see eye to eye with us and made no bones about his liberal outlook. But, as Hendrik said at the time, every man has a right to his own views. There was an old Canon Carlton who had been a great friend of his father's. He was the Rector of a London church and he wrote to us at the time of the engagement and spoke very well of Derek. This good clergyman and his wife seemed to regard Derek almost as a son. But there our information ended. We knew only that he was an attractive personality with a steady job in a well-established British import-export firm and that Lindy and he were very much in love. We never heard mention of his cousin and his wife who were the parents of Lex. Why not? It was only after the adoption that they appeared – posthumously – on the scene. Later, when I pressed Lindy on the subject, she was evasive. In fact, since her return I have found her guarded, no longer the spontaneous forthcoming daughter who left us to go to London two years ago. She won't hear a word of criticism of Lex and declares that if they hadn't adopted this child Mark might never have been born, and Hendrik is inclined to agree. I will say she is a wonderful mother to both children and shows no favouritism towards her own son.

Well, yesterday there was quite a drama here in our home. It's left a curious taste in my mouth and a lot of unanswered questions that Hendrik says are best left alone. 'Don't probe too far, Katie,' he said afterwards. 'Put a knife to certain growths and you only spread the infection.' He knows I'm inquisitive. I worry a problem till I get an answer.

It's Lex who's on my mind. A number of small things buzz around in my head like midges over our fishpond on a summer evening. For instance, quite soon after the family arrived back and before Mark was born, Lindy was having tea with me here one afternoon and Lex was playing on the lawn outside with our bull terrier puppy and I said,

'This cousin of Derek's, what was his name?'

She seemed to have to think for a moment and then she said 'Well Symes, of course. Lex never had to change his name when he came to us. I thought you knew that.'

'I mean his Christian name.'

At once she became impatient and nervous.

'What does it matter? We never talk about his parents. Never! *We* are his parents now. That's all anybody needs to know. An adopted child must be helped to forget his past as quickly and completely as possible. Surely you see that, Mummie?'

I was offended. 'It's just that I'm interested. It seems so extraordinary. Two terrible fatal accidents in one family – Derek's parents and now Lex's. And the child is so remarkably like Derek.'

'It's the relationship. Canon Carlton has photographs of Derek's father and his uncle. They all have the same sort of features.'

But she made an excuse to change the subject. I felt excluded and she hugged me extra warmly when she said good-bye as if to try and make up for hurting me.

Well, yesterday she had some shopping to do in the afternoon and she brought Lex and the baby here while she went into Wynberg. Really, you don't have to go into Cape Town for everything these days. There are excellent shops in the suburban shopping-centres.

'I won't be back much before half-past five,' she said. 'So maybe I'll see Pop then.'

'He should be back by five,' I said. 'He's trying to ease up on his work, but his patients won't let him retire.'

'Of course not, they adore him – and no wonder.'

Then she was gone in her little car and I was left with the children. It didn't really suit me very well to have them just then as my tummy had been upset the day before and I still felt a bit queasy. As a matter of fact I ought to have gone to Veronica Arendse with some dress material she was to make up for me but I'd rung her up and asked her to come to me instead. I'd promised to drive her back. She doesn't really go out sewing any more but she's very obliging and she said as a special favour she'd come out and we could choose the patterns and I could take her back with the material and some other things she was supposed to fit and alter for me. I was expecting her about tea-time. I thought her being there might even turn out handy for Lindy in case she wanted some things run up, but I didn't have a chance to mention it to her. She's always in such a rush these days, never seems to have a moment to spare for a chat before she's off and away.

It was a lovely day. Oh how beautiful these autumn days can be! There's storm and rain in plenty and then suddenly the weather relents and plays at summer. It holds its breath and the leaves lie golden, not even swirling on the wind, and the mountain is lavender against a pure blue sky with wisps of cloud fine as steam. Everybody feels gay, the birds go mad in the bird-bath and if you drive down to the sea the waves are playful too. No thunder of surf. No wonder Lex wanted to play outside, trotting after Samson, the coloured gardener, and teasing Meisie, the dog – though I'd warned him about that. Some bull terriers can be unreliable with children.

I had baby Mark on the sun porch outside my bedroom in his carrycot and from my room I could keep an eye on him and also on Samson and Lex taking barrow-loads of leaves and dead wood to heap on the bonfire near the compost heap, the dog after them. The smell of the fire made me think of picnics and the smoke curled straight up into the still air.

Veronica came punctually at four o'clock. I'd already had my tea and I told her to go to the kitchen and ask Cookie for a cup and a slice of cake before we got busy with my patterns. When she joined me in my bedroom I didn't think she looked very well. She went to the window and she said:

'Your grandsons are here, Mrs van Vuuren. Cookie told me. Shall I go away again? You're probably busy with them.'

'Nonsense,' I said. 'They're no trouble. They won't interfere with us. The baby's in the sun porch. See, he's so good, just playing with his toes, and Lex is out there with Samson.'

We watched them for a moment, Lex's hair bright in the sun. We could hear his shrill voice jabbering in Afrikaans.

'That's something I can't understand,' I said. 'The way he's picked up Afrikaans. He might have spoken it all his life.'

A little muscle was twitching under her eye and she has a funny way of sucking in her cheeks making hollows under those high cheekbones.

'Children imitate wonderfully,' she said. 'Especially noises. Haven't you noticed? They copy noises all the time—animals, cars, aeroplanes, each other, everything. It's why they're so quick at picking up the way people talk – at languages.'

She was watching Lex intently.

167

'When is Mrs Symes coming back to fetch the children?' she asked.

'Around five or a bit later. I'll take you back to your house as soon as she arrives.'

It was quite extraordinary. She seemed to panic. Her voice shook.

'It's not necessary. If that's all the stuff there is – there on your bed – I can carry it. I can get the bus. It's only a step. I must go before five. I have a lot of work waiting at home. We better get on with the fittings now, Mrs van Vuuren.'

I felt she had to drag herself from the window and suddenly I remembered that day at Ann Seymour's when she'd come on to the patio and we'd shown her those coloured snaps of Lex in London – the one with the little Pakistani girl – and she'd said, almost as if she were in a temper, 'What's Lex doing with an Indian girl!' (That had stuck in my mind.) It was so odd. What business was it of hers, anyway? I hadn't been so keen on it myself, if the truth must be known. Nor had Hendrik. But, as we told each other, London was different. Lindy could fraternize with non-Europeans there in a way that would be impossible here. We understand that, of course, even if we can't approve. Here the different races must develop along their own lines in their own separate environment (outside working hours, of course). Friendships would lead to other associations, as we know only too well, and our white population would ultimately become coffee-coloured. Racial purity must be maintained at any cost. Ours is a white man's country and we must keep it so. When and if the Bantusans eventually become independent, we will have to put up with a smaller South Africa but what remains will be ours – white. It's hard to make Derek see our point of view – and we have sometimes thought his influence on Lindy is politically unsound. But Hendrik is not one to interfere. His tolerance is greater than mine.

'We won't discuss these contentious matters,' he says. And I have to respect his wishes.

Veronica had finished pinning the skirts to be altered and we were selecting patterns for the new materials she was going to make up for me when we heard the cry. It was a child's loud piercing yell full of pain and fright. We both rushed to the window.

Lex was lying face down on the lawn and Meisie had her teeth in the back of his leg. Samson was trying to drag her off but she wouldn't let go.

We dashed into the garden and I seized the hose, turned on the tap and hosed the dog's head while Samson succeeded in disengaging her teeth. The bite was deep and bleeding freely and Lex was yelling blue murder.

'He teased the dog,' explained Samson. 'He pulled her tail and she turned on him.'

He lifted the child and carried him into Hendrik's

study. Just then I heard my husband's car and the toot-toot signal he always gives when he gets home. I said to Samson 'Go quickly and tell Master there's been an accident. Tell him what's happened and ask him to hurry.'

Veronica had seated herself in Hendrik's big leather chair and she had taken the screaming child on her lap. I saw that he was all right with her and I dashed out after Samson to meet my husband.

When we entered the study Lex had his face buried against Veronica's breast and his screams had turned to sobs. Tears were pouring unchecked down the girl's face which was ashen, but she only patted the boy as he clung to her and spoke little words of comfort in Afrikaans.

Hendrik looked at her in surprise (the coloureds are very emotional) then he knelt and examined the bite.

'It needs a few stitches,' he said.

He took a syringe from his instrument case, cleaned a place above the wound and gave Lex such a quick injection that he hardly knew what was happening. Then he instructed me how to help him in cleansing and stitching the wound while Veronica still held Lex to her. Gradually her own tears ceased to flow and by the time the injury was bound up both she and the child were calm. I left them in the study while I went to fetch Mark in, for as soon as the sun sets it grows cold and it was already near five o'clock and long

wintry shadows were falling. I lit a fire in the sitting-
room and took the baby's carrycot there. Just then
Lindy's little car skidded to a stop on the gravel drive
outside and she leapt out and up the steps and into the
sitting-room.

'I got everything done early. So here I am to relieve
you of the children. Where's Lex?'

'He had an accident. Meisie bit him.' I felt bad that
he had come to harm in my care. 'Pop has just stitched
up the gash and Lex is in the study sleeping after the
injection – cuddled up on Veronica's lap.'

She had already turned to go to the study but now
she wheeled round in the doorway as if my last words
had lassoed her.

'Veronica! Did you say *Veronica*?'

'Yes. The sewing-girl. She doesn't usually come to
people's houses any more, but she came this afternoon
specially to oblige me. She was here when it happened
and she was very good with Lex. She held him in her
lap while Pop fixed him up.'

She didn't say another word to me, just crossed the
passage to the study with her face set. Hendrik had
gone to wash his hands and I was alone in the sitting-
room. I started to follow Lindy but when she shut the
study door behind her I hesitated.

Lindy has a very clear sweet voice. It carries like a
bell and I couldn't help overhearing what went on. I
think she must have been leaning against the door and I

could picture her looking down at Veronica, her eyes cold as steel.

'You promised,' she was saying. 'You promised you'd never never *never* try to see him.'

'Hush,' said Veronica. 'He's asleep.'

'You promised!'

'I didn't come for that reason. I came to oblige your mother. I had no idea Lex would be here.' The girl's tone was upset and tense but she kept her voice low. 'Though I suppose really it was partly that I wanted to hear somebody talk about him. Your mother —'

'Never do this again. Never as long as you live. Did he recognize you?'

'No, he didn't. He was yelling his head off when the gardener carried him in here and put him in my lap. He never once looked at my face. He was thinking of himself – his fright and pain. He was full of tears.'

'But you held him —'

Veronica's voice was louder now, defiant as she cut in.

'And comforted him. He burrowed his face into my breast. Maybe he recognized the heat and smell of my body without knowing it. Maybe it reminded him of the many times he's been hurt when I've been the one to hold him close and comfort him. That's all. I'm not even a woman to him, I'm nothing – just a sensation of loving – to be forgotten when he wakes.'

'Be quiet!' ordered Lindy suddenly. 'My father's coming back. Promise you won't let me find you with Lex again and keep your word! Stay out of our lives. Do it for *his* sake.' She spoke with terrible urgency.

Then Hendrik was whistling as he went down the passage to the study and the door opened and I heard him explaining to Lindy what had happened and telling her to get Lex to bed as soon as possible

So presently we had them all three stowed into Lindy's little car and she was on her way

'I'll look in tomorrow,' her father said. 'Lex'll be all right.'

Afterwards Veronica and I finished our business and she tried to insist on going home by herself.

'I can carry those things,' she persisted. But she looked so shaken I refused to allow it.

'You've had a shock. I'll take you back myself.'

I too had had a shock.

I could make neither head nor tail of the conversation I'd heard between my daughter and Veronica but I had found it horribly disturbing and alarming. Why had Lindy spoken with such bitter fury to a girl who had only tried to help an injured child? Veronica's husky words lingered in my ears. 'I'm nothing – just a sensation of loving – to be forgotten when he wakes.' And the tears raining silently down her pinched cheeks haunted me. Why had she cried so agonizingly in that strange inward fashion as if her very heart were breaking?

It was misty on the de Waal Drive when we turned Hospital Bend, a sea mist that blurred the lights just beginning to prick the dusk round the bay and on the Flats. There was no wind to disperse it.

I had a thousand questions I wanted to ask Veronica but I felt as if any one of them might lead me into a quagmire. She was very quiet and the tension stretched between us unbearably. At last I said,

'You were very worried about Lex. You were crying.'

'I had a queer feeling,' she said.

'What sort of feeling?'

'As if it had all happened before and would happen again – me holding him like that.'

The coloureds are fey at times. One just has to accept that and her words gave me a little cold shiver, but I said,

'Don't be silly. It hasn't happened before and it certainly won't again. We'll get rid of the dog, give her away. There'll be no difficulty finding a home for her, she has a pedigree as long as your arm. Bull terriers and small children don't always go together. I told my husband so, but he's fond of the dog and he didn't want to listen. Now he'll be content to let Meisie go.'

She nodded, and I said,

'You have a little boy of your own, I believe? Mrs Seymour told me.'

'Not any more.'

'What happened to him?'

'He was adopted by an English family.'

'Did you take him to England yourself?'

She didn't answer at once. I knew that she was thinking it out – whether to tell me the truth or a lie. I repeated the question. She passed a hand across her face as if to wipe out a memory.

'I wanted him brought up in England. But if you don't mind, Mrs van Vuuren, I'd rather not talk about it.'

She wasn't rude, just stone wall determined. She killed that catechism beyond revival. But now I remembered that ages ago Ann Seymour had complained that she couldn't get hold of Veronica as she was away overseas. I tried to pinpoint the time. Yes, it was after Ann's return from the Transvaal over two years back. Not very long after Derek and Lindy had settled in London . . .

'We turn up here,' she said. 'To the left.'

'Yes, of course. I remember.'

I'd been to her father's house before when she'd done some work for me, but I'd nearly missed the turning. I'd been making calculations.

I left her at the gate. She gathered the dresses and

material from the back seat and thanked me for the lift home.

'I'll ring you when I'm ready for a fitting,' she said. 'It's better if you come to me. It isn't easy for me to go out —'

'I understand. It was nice of you to come today. It really could have waited.'

'I wanted to come.'

I noticed her small delicate wrists and narrow tapering fingers. Lex had hands like that and there was the same slight upward tilt to the outer corners of his big melting eyes.

'Totsiens,' I said. 'I'll see you soon, Veronica.'

'Good-night, Mrs van Vuuren. I hope Lex will soon be quite well again.'

I drove home with my mind in a tumult. Pieces of a very strange and shocking jigsaw were falling inexorably into place. For the first time in our married life I knew that here was something vitally important that I would rather have concealed from my husband. If what I feared was true he would find it very difficult to forgive Derek or understand Lindy. Our family might well be split from top to toe and our only daughter entirely lost to us. Lindy had taken her stand for her own reasons and nothing could call back or alter what had already been done. Yet I knew, as I sat at the wheel in the gathering dusk, that I would not be able to keep my fears and surmises from Hendrik. Down the years we have become one – two halves of a whole. A doctor sees so much more of human beings than the ailing bodies he tries to heal, he comes to know what is important and what is trivial (women seldom discriminate and keep a balance) and now I felt a great need of Hendrik's wisdom.

One thing is sure. If my suspicions are justified no good can come of what has happened to these two young people and their little Lex. But it may be many years before a harvest of inevitable tragedy is reaped. When that day comes – if we are still here – Lindy must be able to count on us – her father and mother.

# 16

## JOHN BURFORD

*'It was torture, Mr Burford!'*

Lindy telephoned me in something very like panic. It was eight in the evening and I was just about to go over to my neighbours to make up a four at bridge.

'John,' she said. 'There's been a new development since we saw you last night.'

Her vibrant voice was pitched a note higher than usual and there was a tremor in it.

'The hunchback?'

'No. Veronica. Derek and I are both worried.'

She told me Lex had been bitten by the van Vuuren's bull terrier and Veronica had been in the house at the time and it was she who had held him in her arms and soothed him while Dr van Vuuren put in the stitches.

'Did he recognize her?'

'She says not. She says he was too upset to know who was who or what was what. But he clung to her —'

'If he didn't recognize her surely there's nothing to worry about. Has he talked of her?'

'No. What bothers me is the fact of her going to my

178

mother's house at all. She doesn't go out to work now. She works at home and has a Malay girl to help her. Yet she made an exception for Mummie. Why? *Why*, John? Obviously she hoped to see Lex – and she promised us she'd never try to see him. Not ever! Don't you understand how this makes me feel? Unsafe – surrounded – as if all the past we've buried was rising up to harm us and trap Lex. First the hunchback, now Veronica. Why can't we be shot of all that?'

'Does Derek feel this way about it too?'

'Yes. We both do. Can you stop her? Can you forbid her to work for my mother?'

I love Lindy – let's face it – I love her, but I was suddenly very impatient.

'You're crazy. What would your mother think if Veronica suddenly threw in her hand and refused to sew for her? What would Ann Seymour think? They're friends. Mrs van Vuuren got hold of Veronica through Ann. You told me so yourself and you said how lucky it was Veronica worked at home. That way she'd never be likely to see Lex.'

'But now she has!'

'This was an isolated occasion. I can try to make sure it doesn't happen again that way. But I certainly can't dictate to your mother who is to sew for her and who isn't. Nor can you. Now simmer down and take it easy.'

'You'll do something, John? Say you will.'

'I'll do something. Leave it to me with the other business – the hunchback. And relax, Lindy.'

'Bless you.' Her voice was calmer and I could hear her sigh of relief.

I had a few words with Derek and told him to calm Lindy down and then I went off to bridge. One hand I revoked and my partner, who was also my hostess, laughed and said, 'You simply aren't with us this evening. You're in love, my friend, and high time too – though I prefer my men friends single.'

So there I was again with more dirty work to be done for Derek and Lindy. I found myself burning with the old futile resentment against Derek. Yet I knew I wasn't being fair to him. He'd come to South Africa as a stranger – very young, very incredulous of our fantastic apartheid laws that obtain nowhere else in the world, he'd overstepped one of them and he'd never stopped paying the price. The damnable part was the way Lindy had got sucked into the whole mess-up. She was spinning round in a whirlpool of deception that seemed never-ending. Neither for Derek, herself, Veronica and most of all Lex.

Poor little devil. Even if he weathered the storm till manhood he'd then be up against the worst problem of the lot. What is one white infusion in a sea of dark blood? Fair enough, there have clearly been other white progenitors in his family, many of them, but the brown is strong, God knows, and it would be strange if Lex, even with a lily-white mate, failed to breed at least one child who would be an outcast in the South African white world into which he's been pitched by Veronica's iron will. How often we see that tragedy! The brown child with crimpy hair, classified white because his parents are accepted as white, and then when he goes to a government school he's expelled because the white parents threaten to withdraw their little darlings if a child 'obviously coloured' is allowed to stay and associate with them. Such children have to receive private tuition. What a traumatic experience for both child and parents!

Meanwhile there was this problem of the boy and the dwarf – to say nothing of Veronica. It was obvious that Jacobs was intent upon establishing a relationship with Lex for no good purpose. I sent a messenger to his house with a note suggesting that he meet me at my flat on the following Sunday morning. If that was impossible he was to ring me at the office. I heard nothing so I assumed – rightly – that he would show up. It was my purpose to put the wind up him. My contacts with him had been brief and if he'd been getting a rake off from Veronica on Derek's payments that was their business. But since the adoption all that was finished. The whole affair had been washed up and it was over two years since I had seen Jacobs or Veronica.

The hunchback turned up at my flat at eleven o'clock on the dot. The maid, who just comes in for half an hour on Sunday mornings to tidy up in a slapdash way, had gone and we were alone.

I had forgotten how short he was, a squat figure with a large head, a barrel chest and muscular arms. He crossed the room with his surprisingly light tread as if on springs and went straight out on to the balcony and looked enviously at the sea.

'I was a night-watchman in flats by the sea,' he said in Afrikaans. 'That was when Mr Symes was living at Three Anchor Bay.'

'I know. Sit down, Jacobs, we must talk.'

I indicated a chair on the balcony and he sat nervously on the edge of it. I gave him a cigarette and a box of matches and watched him light up. I filled a pipe myself. The air was cold but the sun sparkled on the sea and the smell of salt and seaweed was astringent. The Atlantic rollers raced for the shore, swelling green and bursting in gigantic lines of surf and spray. It was high tide.

I took a seat and drew hard on my pipe.

'Now,' I said, sticking to Afrikaans. 'What's this I hear about you hanging round Mr Symes's place and talking to Lex?'

His eyes evaded mine. They were small and cunning, the yellowish whites red-veined. He was dark skinned and ugly but his face was not particularly unpleasant.

He wouldn't normally scare a modern child accustomed to the grotesque in toys and pictures. I wondered how old he was. It was impossible to tell. Thirty, forty?

'Veronica wants to know how her son is getting on,' he said in his quick explosive way.

'You know as well as I do that Veronica has no more claim to Lex. That was the way she wanted it and that's the way she's got it. He's her son no longer.'

'She likes to have news of him.'

'The news of him is good. She has nothing to worry about. He does well at school, his health is fine, his parents are kind to him and he loves them. What more can she ask?'

'She asks that I see him every now and again and tell her how he is.'

'I don't believe you. When Lex was adopted Veronica begged Mrs Symes to tell the child that she was dead. Dead, I tell you! She wanted to wash the slate clean of his beginnings. Lex is to be left alone. You are never to try to see him again. You are part of the life Veronica wants him to forget.'

'Perhaps *I* want him to remember.'

He was leaning forward, his coarse face smiling, amiably enough. His bloodshot gaze fixed mine. I suspected that he found my brand of cigarettes tame and preferred rolling his own reefers.

'Lex is no affair of yours.'

'I am interested in Lex.'

'Why?'

'I have six children – another since last I saw you, Mr Burford – and no work. I live on occasional odd jobs. I need money for my family. Even coloured people must eat.'

So here it came – the threat.

He stubbed out his cigarette with powerful blunt fingers.

'If I am not to see Lex I must be paid to keep away.'

Now was my moment for turning the screw.

'If you molest that child again the police will be informed.'

He laughed. It was an insolent sound, as raucous as the gulls mewing round the flats.

'The police would be interested to know about Lex – and Veronica and the boy's father.'

It was a cold day but I felt the sweat start out on my forehead.

'Mr Symes holds a British passport, his wife naturally has one too. The child was legally adopted in England. He is not a South African child any more.'

'The Immorality Act is not only for South Africans. It is for everybody in this country. It is the law. The police are interested in people who have broken the law. We brown people know that only too well. If a white man has a coloured wife – even if they were married long before the Immorality Act was law – they must part. The law is the law. Veronica broke it with her white man and they can still be sentenced for what they did.'

Everything he said was jerky, disjointed and terribly to the point. Why had I thought him stupid as well as deformed? I had paid him perfunctorily on Derek's account month after month and I had never properly observed him or held a conversation with him. I had assumed he was 'safe'. Veronica had said so. Now I saw the shrewd triumphant gleam in his inflamed eyes.

'You can prove nothing,' I said, but my mouth felt dry.

'Lex is not a boy people forget. There are many in our neighbourhood who don't like Veronica. She thinks she's too good for us. I know people who would like to prove he was her child. And am I myself not proof? I passed her the money you gave me for her child's support. Also Lex remembers me. If I take him to District Six he will remember his home and his oupa and his mother. He will betray himself and his parents.'

He put his hand out to the cigarette-box and I nodded.

'Help yourself.'

I sprang to my feet and went to the parapet and stood there with my back to Jacobs, breathing deeply in an attempt to control a choking upsurge of red rage. At that moment it was directed less against the hunchback than against Derek. The silly selfish bloody fool! How dared he think he could break the law of the land and get away with it! Why a coloured girl – *why*? He could have had white ones for free, these days who cares? But no, he doesn't want an emotional entanglement so he walks into a trap. Then, without a word of warning to her, he drags Lindy into it too. Deep in, and adds the child to the sordid picture. That moment, with the blood pounding in my ears like the surf on the rocks, I had murder in my heart. So this young Englishman – my friend – comes here to the Cape and he doesn't believe in apartheid and he's hot for a brown girl and he gets it out of his system, and after that he takes my girl – my clean lovely Lindy – and smears the tar across her life while he laughs and sweeps her off her feet into a marriage risky from the word go. I found my fists clenched and my jaw set. I was shocked at the force of my own emotions. Now, for the first time, I saw Lindy's future as seriously threatened and that was all that mattered to me.

The hunchback, smoking quietly behind me, was almost forgotten. He was only a symptom of the greater evil. He was the parasite. Derek and Veronica were the guilty ones. Let them get out of this dirty mess as best they could! I'd have no more to do with it. Yet they needed me still – now more than ever. For Lindy's sake I knew I'd get bogged down with them, however I might feel about it. Why fight the fact? I drew a long breath to clear my head of the fury that I realized was unjust, and swung round to face Jacobs.

'What do you want? What money are you trying to extort?'

'The money Mr Symes paid Veronica regularly for Lex. That money. He can pay *me* now. That's all I want. He has a good job. I have none.'

'Then get one! Give up dagga and try work. You've gone sour, you runt!'

His face darkened. He was on his feet, no higher than my waist.

'I'll take twenty rand now,' he said.

'You'll take nothing from me,' I said. 'You'll do your own dirty work with Mr Symes. I'll have no more part in this business.'

He grinned, showing discoloured broken teeth.

'Good. I'll go to his house. If he isn't there I can talk to Mrs Symes.'

I counted twenty rand out of my wallet and slapped them on to the small table at his elbow.

'Take the notes,' I said furiously. 'And keep away from Mr Symes's home and his wife and children. He'll get in touch with you.'

'Soon?'

'Soon. Now, get out!'

I shot ahead of him and opened the flat door. He stepped lightly past me, shabby, deformed, smelling of unwashed flesh and the pungent tang of dagga, muttering to himself. I slammed the door behind him, sickened, revolted, wondering what the hell next.

Next was obvious. I must find out from Veronica how dangerous this human skunk really was. And I must make sure that she'd keep out of Lex's way in future.

I drove up to District Six that same evening about 7.30, but the Arendse house was locked and shuttered. Veronica and her father had evidently gone to church. Strangely enough, the churches are always packed there among the poor. They wear their best clothes and really listen to the sermons. Most of them have faith and God knows they need the dream of a paradise to come. So I parked outside the deserted schoolhouse and waited for them to return. The evening was cold and windless and I watched the nightly miracle of more and more clusters and garlands and ribbons of light blossoming in the city, the bay and across the Flats. It was Fairyland indeed and no doubt it was here that the hunchback meant to bring Lex when he said 'Snow white boy, I will take you to Fairyland.' Poor little snow white coloured boy, child of two worlds, unconscious of his origin!

It was near eight when I saw them walking up the hill, Mr Arendse in his neat dark suit and Veronica in a cherry coloured coat with a little velvet cap to match on her black hair. In spite of the vivid colour she appeared demure, almost austere, as if the atmosphere of the church still lingered about her. Sanctuary. Well, I'd soon be jerking her out of that!

As they drew abreast of the car I got out and greeted them.

'I need to talk to Veronica,' I said.

Mr Arendse frowned and shifted the angle of his spectacles.

'We have friends coming in —'

'This is urgent,' I insisted. 'I won't keep her long. Let me take her for a short drive.'

She said bitterly. 'Wherever a car parks with a white man and a coloured girl in it a policeman pops up out of the earth.'

'We needn't park.'

She made up her mind suddenly.

'I'll come.' She turned to her father. 'I'll be back in time to make coffee. The sandwiches are ready – under a damp cloth in the kitchen.'

He didn't argue but he seemed worried and displeased as she climbed in beside me.

I drove down to Woodstock and headed towards Bloubergstrand. The marshes and hills over that way were in moonlight. They had a phantom look.

'It's the hunchback,' I said. 'He's trying to blackmail Derek.'

'Oh, God!' She made a fist and pressed her knuckles against her mouth. 'I was scared of that.'

'What's happened to him? I thought you said he was safe.'

'A while ago he tried to make love to me. Mad fool! He's been smoking dagga. He thought he was a god. There are women who go for dwarfs. Did you know that? I'm not one of them. Danie Jacobs has a woman now – not his wife. He needs money to keep her. She's bad and she's got him mixed up in all sorts of rackets instead of working respectably. When they find out something wrong about a person they start putting on the heat. Asking for money. Getting it.'

'How much does this woman know about you?'

'Nothing definite. Danie wouldn't tell her because she'd expect a share of the money. She might even use the information herself. Danie's sly. He doesn't want that.'

The moon on sea and strand was silver, the lines of surf shone here and there with the glimmering glow of phosphorous.

'Did you know Jacobs had been hanging round the Symes's place, talking to Lex, trying to lure him away? "To Fairyland" he said – telling the child there was someone in Fairyland wanting to see him.'

She was silent. I glanced at her blunt pretty profile, the lips pouting, the brow furrowed. 'He told me you'd put him up to it – that you wanted him to see the boy – to get news of him.'

She shook her head. 'It's a lie. Lex is a white child

190

now. That's what I wanted. He must never be mixed
up with any of us.' Oh, yes? I thought. But I decided
to leave that matter till later.

'Just the same, Jacobs is trying to get the boy into
his power.'

'I can imagine it.' She was concentrating deeply,
trying to put herself into the hunchback's astute and
avaricious mind. 'If he can go to Derek and tell him
that Lex knows us Danie can threaten to take the next
step of finding people who remember the boy and
who'll be interested to learn he's not in England at all –
adopted over there like I said – but right here! People
don't forget a child like Lex easily. If they start talking
they can make it simple for Danie to prove Derek is the
father and I am the mother. Then the police can get us
for contravening the Immorality Act – no matter that
it happened years ago. They're doing it all the time – to
high up people, even professors and clergymen, *anyone*
who's ever broken that law. Danie Jacobs can make
Derek pay and pay, don't you see? And, if Derek re-
fuses, the pig can have his revenge and give us away
to the authorities.'

She was talking in agitated rushes.

'It's Lex I'm thinking of, not Derek or me. Danie can
ruin Lex's whole life.' She broke off, half in tears.

'Fairyland —' she added. 'The lights of Cape Town
and the Flats . . . we always said they were Fairyland.
Lex really believed it. Danie Jacobs knows that.'

'So you're pretty sure Jacobs means to take him – home? Prod his memory?'

'I suppose so. He's out to make trouble.'

'And money?'

'He needs money for that greedy woman. As well as for his family. He's gone rotten like fruit left too long in the sun.'

She knew it so well. People could do that – go rotten. Dagga saw to that.

The bones of Table Mountain and Lion's Head and Devil's Peak loomed over us, X-rayed by moonlight. District Six was part of the glittering pattern of the city in the lap of the great solid old mountain. Vice, despair and filth were hidden by the 'suit of lights' the coloured quarter assumed after dark when the knife and other weapons of evil flashed and struck in the narrow lanes.

'Have you tried to see the boy since his return?' I asked.

'No,' she said in a low broken voice. 'I love him too much for that. I am dead to him. We are all dead to him – the coloured people he used to know.'

'His parents love him as much as you do. And he loves them. He has no home other than theirs, no life beyond the life they give him. They have kept their part of the bargain faithfully. But I hear from Mrs Symes that you are not keeping yours.'

'What did Mrs Symes tell you?' she asked defensively.

'That you went to Mrs van Vuuren's house – no doubt in the hope of seeing Lex – that when he was bitten by the dog it was you who held him in your lap. If he hadn't been so frightened and upset he would unquestionably have recognized you.'

'I did go to Mrs van Vuuren. She begged me to because she had been sick and it suited her better than coming to me. But I didn't hope to see Lex – only to hear of him. I know now that I ought to have refused to go to her house. It was dangerous. I will never do it again. I'd hoped to get news of him, perhaps see photos of him —'

'You can get news of him if she comes to you.'

Suddenly she turned on me fiercely.

'Do you think it was easy for me to hold that boy against my breast, to see him suffer, to be so close to him, so part of him, and yet not let him know who I was? It was torture, Mr Burford! It was death.'

Her voice broke and tears poured down her face. She fumbled in her bag for a handkerchief and her light gloves were darkened with the great drops that fell on them.

'He's all right now,' I said more gently. 'Don't feel anxious. But be careful to spare yourself and to spare him the danger of meeting you face to face. It mustn't happen. Never again.'

'I've said that – and I mean it.'

She choked over the words and we were silent the

rest of our way back to her father's house. Gradually she became composed. As a matter of fact, she seemed oblivious when I stopped outside her home. She sat there, her face stony, a little muscle twitching under her left eye. Her hands, still gloved, were tightly clasped in her lap and her soft full lips were set in a hard line.

I leaned across her and opened the door. The gesture and its implication released her from a spell. She picked up her bag from the seat where it had been lying and prepared to get out.

'Good-night, Mr Burford,' she said. 'Thank you for telling me what has been happening. I must think about the dwarf. There is a lot to think about. I must see him – tell him to lay off – or else . . .'

I watched her walk the little distance from the school-house to her home, back straight, buttocks swaying. They can't help it, they all have that special tart's come-on wiggle, even the best of them. But I wasn't thinking of her supple body then, I was thinking of her ravaged face when she spoke of the child and wept and of her hard implacable expression when she mentioned the dwarf. Danie Jacobs, who had once been an ally, had become an enemy. Her child's future was at stake – his white future. Veronica wouldn't see that wrecked if she could help it.

# 17

# LINDY

*'In this hour . . . Lex was entirely Veronica's'*

John Burford came to our house on the Sunday night
after he'd seen Veronica. It must have been after nine.
He hadn't had anything to eat and I made him some
sandwiches but he wasn't hungry. Derek gave him a
whisky and soda. Minnie was out, the children were
asleep and we were alone. We'd been watering the
garden earlier and we were still in slacks and rather
untidy.

He reassured us about Veronica but what he told us
about the hunchback frightened me.

'Blackmail! That can go on for ever —'

'Yes,' he said sharply. 'And I've had enough of the
whole business. I wash my hands of it. Now it's all over
to you, Derek – where it rightly belongs.'

Derek's mobile face, so quick to laughter, was grim.

'Fair enough. I'll see Jacobs when I get back from
Johannesburg.'

'What's this about Johannesburg?' John asked.

'One of our London directors is here at present and

I'm to go with him to Johannesburg tomorrow, and then on to Durban and Port Elizabeth. I'll be back here at the end of the week. It'll all be pretty hectic.'

John lit his pipe, then he said, 'If I were you I'd try for a transfer. Johannesburg, Durban, London, any other branch. Get out of Cape Town.'

'But we love it here!' I cried. 'What would Mummie and Pop say if we were suddenly moved?'

John shrugged. 'You've got tangled up in the machinery of apartheid. The worst possible way, the deeply human way —'

'It's fanatic – it's bloody well incredible!' Derek had helped himself to a drink and his hand shook as he raised his glass. 'Where else in the world could you find a goddamn situation like this? Nowhere, but nowhere!'

'You find it here. You were warned. You knew what you were doing at the time and then you dragged Lindy into it!'

John's eyes were blazing as he looked at Derek. My heart turned over. That was the way my father would feel if he found out the truth about Lex. And I would be condemned and despised for my connivance. As for the child – our clever affectionate little boy – he would be an outcast.

Derek stared at his friend who seemed suddenly to have become his foe. Anger flamed in his face, died and gave way to bewilderment.

'It all happened so long ago. Nearly seven years ago. It wasn't a crime —'

'In our country it *was* a crime – a criminal offence. Oh, you needn't look at me like that! I didn't make the law. I don't necessarily approve of it, though God knows I'd respect it. The fact is you're as guilty now as you were then – same as if you'd committed murder – and you're stuck with the consequences. So is Lex, poor little devil. One day you'll have to tell him everything and then what's he up against? He too will have to decide whether he wants a marriage based on a secret – vulnerable to blackmail. And what of his children? As for Lindy, she suffers for all of you.'

I had never heard John talk with such vehement bitterness, his voice so clipped and taut I felt it might break at any moment.

'I was a fool and a coward,' he went on. 'I ought to have told Lindy that you were marrying her with this – *thing* – on your conscience. I was afraid she'd hate me for the rest of my life if I told her the truth. But what did that matter, anyway? I should have told her. It was my duty.'

He got up and left us without so much as a good-night.

Derek turned to me. 'So our bloody best friend is still in love with you!'

He ran his hands through his hair.

'I'd like to try for a transfer as John suggested. It's the obvious answer but how the hell can I ask the directors to shift me out of a plum job – to demote me – without giving them a valid reason? And there's no valid reason they'd understand. It just isn't on. They've done me proud and I ought to be licking their shoes in gratitude, not bleating for an office somewhere else.'

'You can't,' I said. 'I don't want you to. We'll weather this thing together somehow – here. After what John told us I don't believe Veronica will risk trying to see Lex. She loves him too much. As for the hunchback, we'll tackle that somehow when you come back from your tour. If necessary we'll have to keep paying him off . . .'

He came and took my shoulders in his big hands and I felt his long fingers hard on the bones. Gripping, compulsive.

'Oh, Lindy, Lindy, what have I let you in for?'

I looked up into his intense tawny eyes and saw the carved nostrils expanding, the springing copper hair like Lex's. I shrugged. He felt the movement of negation.

'You blame me so much? You too?'

'There's no end to it,' I said sadly. 'It just goes on and on.'

'You could forgive me once. You did.'

'But I'm not allowed to forget.'

'So you have to forgive me afresh – again and again?'

'Don't talk about forgiving, Derek. We can't judge each other. We are as we are and what's done is done. We can't rewrite our lives to make happy endings.'

'I love you. I've never thought twice about anybody else since I met you.'

'And I love you. But I love Lex too. I only wish to God he were mine and not Veronica's. Then he'd be safe.'

He bent his head and his cheek was against mine. He held me tight and everything that was unsaid between us was known and understood – the loving and the forgiving and the ever-increasing fear.

How I wish that I could tell my mother everything – that we could sit by the fire together and thrash it all out. There was a time when I used to take her all my problems, when I was confident that there'd never be a problem too cruel for her to face with me. Yet here is something she'd never understand. She might try but she'd never really be able to comprehend how Derek could do what he did – or, if she did, she wouldn't forgive. I remember when I began to expand my ideas at Varsity she fought them. So did Pop. They didn't mind my studying Social Science but they hated the practical side of it – the contacts we students made with the non-Europeans in their miserable settlements down

on the Flats – the pondokkie areas that were being
rebuilt and resettled and the people rehabilitated in
every way. In his time as a student Pop had worked in
the Flats clinics organized and staffed by medical
students, but he didn't fancy that sort of thing for me –
'a young girl'. He doesn't know that our generation is
tough and real and honest, that we see wrongs and
want to right them and evils that arise out of poverty-
stricken environment and that we believe we can
really help, apart from collecting money as the
universities always do anyway.

I think it was when we mulled these things over
together that my parents and I began to grow a little
apart. A great many of us students wanted to be able
to fraternize with our non-European fellow students
on and off the campus and we resented the Government interference that insisted on no joint social
activities. My parents agreed with the Government. I
suppose, if they knew about Derek, they'd say 'Now,
Lindy, you understand *why*. You see what can happen
when young people of different races are thrown
together.' And, if they knew that I didn't condemn my
husband or despise his child, they'd still be more
convinced of the rightness of their own views. Derek
and I would both be past salvation and Lex an object
of profound pity.

All this makes me feel I'm in a trap. Even John
doesn't like being drawn into the web fate is spinning

closer and closer around us. I have heaps of friends and yet, at times like this, I feel terribly alone – and afraid.

Derek left for Johannesburg with his London boss on Monday and I expected him back at the end of the week. On Thursday John took me out to dinner. I was all wrought up. The matter of the hunchback was in abeyance till Derek's return and I didn't trust that potential blackmailer an inch. But there was nothing to be done for the time being. Since John had opted out, I made up my mind not to talk to him on the subject but to keep my fears to myself.

The evening was cold and bright and full of stars. It is like that at this season – days and nights of unimaginable beauty and serenity sandwiched between rain, high winds and violent storms. Sometimes it seems to me that my marriage has become like that – a few golden hours here and there, islanded between periods of great turbulence.

When John came for me I was just tucking up Mark and Lex. Now that it is too late, I know that I ought to have guessed there was trouble afoot when I kissed Lex good night. He hugged me as if he would never let me go. I disengaged his little hands from my neck.

'I'm going out with John now. Minnie will be here to take care of you and I shan't be late. When I come in I'll peep at you and Mark.'

He looked mischievous and chuckled. 'Will Minnie sit in the kitchen?'

'I expect so. She usually does. She has her radio for company. Now, tell me, what are you going to dream about? Something beautiful?'

He nodded vigorously. 'I'm going to dream about Fairyland.'

'That'll be nice.'

Nothing warned me, no premonition. Yet now those laughing black eyes haunt me. The message was there and I failed to read it. I can still feel my hands loosening his grip from my neck, I can smell the sweet sleepy warmth of him as I kissed him good-night. I turned off the light and he said 'Bye-bye, Mommie,' and I answered 'God bless you, darling.' It was all so normal.

John was waiting for me by the fire. He had mixed me a martini. He had a bottle of red wine with him because we were going to the Steak Cavern and they have no liquor licence.

'Do you know the Steak Cavern telephone number?' I asked.

'I've got it here in my little book.'

John took his small red engagement diary from his pocket and read out the number. I scribbled it on a piece of paper.

'For Minnie – just in case. I always leave her our telephone number when we go out.'

He laughed. 'You're a conscientious mother, aren't you?'

'Well, after all, one never knows.'

Before we left I went into the kitchen. Fat old Minnie heaved herself up out of her rocker as I entered. When she is baby-sitting she always brings it into the kitchen for greater comfort. I gave her the piece of paper with the telephone number on it.

She took it and threw me a smiling glance of appraisal.

'Meddem looks nice in that dress.'

It was simple but the colour was good – a sort of periwinkle-blue wool that goes well with my eyes.

'Leave the kitchen door ajar so you can hear if Mark cries. We'll be back by half-past nine – before Mark wakes up anyway so I can give him his ten o'clock feed. Don't forget to bolt the front door after us.'

If she bolted the door on the inside Minnie knew she'd have to wait up for us. And that was fair enough. We didn't go out all that often, and we made it up to her one way or another when we did.

The Steak Cavern is at Sea Point. There the air was even sharper and the rollers were crashing in, enormous after the storm of the day before. The stars were tiny icicles in the purple-indigo sky. Inside the Steak Cavern it was warm and smelt of the grill and the lights were dim except for the counter where the chef in his high white cap turned the meat over the glowing coals. Our table was in a corner. Secluded. I slipped my fur off my shoulders on to the back of my chair.

'I love you in furs,' said John. 'They make you look very fair and northern – an ice maiden.'

'An ice maiden. That's good.' Every so often he shoots an old-fashioned romantic line and I have to debunk him.

He grinned and we turned our attention to the menu. We ordered prawn cocktails and tournedos. The waiter took the chill off the red wine. We talked of everything except the problems uppermost in my mind. John made me laugh. He even made me forget.

It must have been near nine o'clock when the telephone rang and the waiter came over to our table.

'Mrs Symes, your maid wants to speak to you. If you'll come this way.'

The telephone was next to the cashier's desk. I picked up the receiver with apprehension. Minnie's voice was shrill and agitated.

'Meddem, it's Lex. He's gone!'

'Gone? Where?' My heart turned over and the wine was sour in my throat.

'I don't know. I went to look if the children was all right and Lex's bed was empty. I thought he might be hiding but then I saw a chair by the front door. He must've got up on it and pulled the bolt open.'

'You'd have heard him —'

'No, my wireless was playing. I didn't hear nothing. I don't know when he went. His slippers and his dressing-gown is missing too.'

'Hold on, Minnie. I'll call Mr Burford.'

'I'm here, Lindy.'

I turned, trembling, to see John standing behind me. He took the receiver from me and questioned Minnie.

'Did you hear a car in the lane? Or voices?'

'No, sir, my wireless was on.'

'Go and feel if his bed is still warm.'

There was a pause. When she came on the line again her voice was calmer.

'Yes, he can't have been gone long.'

'I think we can find him, Minnie. Just go back to Mark and wait for us.'

'Hold on!' I said, to John. 'I must speak to Minnie again.' I took the instrument from him. 'If Mark wakes and cries, Minnie, give him his bottle, change him and put him down again. If he's quiet don't wake him. I'll attend to him myself when I get home.'

'Yes, Meddem.'

I hung up and turned to John. His face was grave. My own must have been ghastly because he took my arm as if to support me.

'Lindy, you realize that Jacobs, the hunchback, is probably – almost certainly – behind this.'

'Yes, Lex said he was going to dream about Fairyland. He must have met Jacobs deliberately. It must have been prearranged. It's some sort of plot. It's kidnapping —'

He took both my shaking hands in one of his. His grip was firm and steady.

'We'll go at once.'

'But where?'

'To the Arendse house. My bet is that he's taken Lex to Veronica. He wants the boy to recognize his early surroundings – people, perhaps. If Lex reacts, Jacobs will be in a position to turn the screw on Derek later. This may be embarrassing but there's no reason to think Lex has come to harm.'

'People snatch children and hold them to ransom . . . in dreadful places under awful conditions.'

I felt the tears well into my eyes as I thought of my trusting little Lex who'd go off with anyone anywhere, laughing, chattering, putting his small confiding hand into that of the hunchback who'd promised to show him Fairyland. Utterly unsuspecting.

John paid the waiter and said, 'I'm sorry we have to rush away. We'll come again soon.'

When we were in the car he flung his arm about my shoulders and gave me a brief hug.

'Don't cry, Lindy. Please, darling. It's going to be all right.'


It can't have taken us much more than ten minutes to get from the Steak Cavern in Sea Point to the Arendse house in District Six but it seemed an eternity.

I'd never been in District Six before. We wound up

the long hill in low gear. Lights burned and candles flickered in the narrow flat-roofed houses, men argued and gambled on the pavements and women strolled in pairs or loitered invitingly under the street lamps with heavily painted faces and skirts scarcely below their thighs, children romped and quarrelled in the gutters where once my son, Lex, had played. Below us, under the dark mass of Table Mountain, the shimmering lights fanned out round the curve of the bay and away and beyond, reaching into the hinterland.

Towards the top of the hill the street turned in a sort of S bend. John drew up by the darkened empty schoolhouse. On the opposite side of the road a small battered Austin stood near an open gate.

'That's the house, and my guess is that the car outside it belong to Jacobs. Wait here, Lindy, and I'll investigate!'

It was quiet right up there at the upper end of the street. No one was about. John went and inspected the car and within a few moments he was back.

'That's Jacobs's car all right. The pedals are raised and the seat is right forward. Only an exceptionally short person could drive it. I'm going in to the house. I think it's best for you to stay here. The less you're mixed up in this the better. Leave it to me. If you're nervous sound the horn.'

It wasn't dark where we had parked under a street lamp, but my impulse was to go with him. *If only I had!*

Instead I watched him hurry across the road and walk quickly towards the open gate. After that everything happened very fast.

A sudden shaft of orange light slanted outwards as the house door opened and a little figure in a dressing-gown dashed out into the night. He dodged as John tried to catch him and a girl ran after the fleeing child. I sprang out of the car and round the bonnet.

'Lex!' I cried. 'Lex!' Anything to stop that headlong rush!

He hesitated and turned his head.

'Mommie!' His voice was distraught, choked with tears.

He swerved off the pavement and charged into the road to cross to me. He looked neither right nor left. The beam of head lamps rounded the S turn as a lorry came down the hill. There was the grinding squeal of brakes and the shriek of heavy double tyres as the driver skidded in a desperate attempt to avoid the child.

The small running form was caught in the beam like a frantic animal and I stood stricken and helpless as the tall radiator crashed into the little copper head and brought Lex down. When the lorry came to a halt he was sprawled on the ground behind it. He lay like a rag doll thrown down by a careless child, bloodied and crushed in the glare of the red rear lights.

John and I reached him at the same time and then

Veronica too was on her knees beside him. Her arms slipped under him and without a word she lifted him and carried him into her home. So great was her authority at that moment, so supreme her right to move him from the cold wintry street that none of us uttered a single protest.

In this hour of disaster Lex was entirely Veronica's.

# 18

## LUTHER ARENDSE

*'You don't know this white child'*

It was so peaceful, that cold winter evening, just Veronica and me in our pleasant front room with the electric radiator to warm us and the lights full on because she was cutting out a dress for one of her ladies.

She had the stuff – some lavender silk – spread on the rug and the paper pattern pinned on top of it and she was kneeling, snipping away confidently with her big sharp cutting-out scissors. She's clever and industrious and I only wish she'd settle for that nice young builder who wants to marry her but she can't seem to make up her mind. That business with Derek Symes was a tragedy. She had really loved him and, as for the child he was still everything in the world to her.

She'd told me about Danie Jacobs that Sunday night when Mr Burford met us after church. 'Danie's been blackmailing Derek Symes. He hangs around the Symes's place trying to make friends with Lex. I've

warned him to leave Lex alone, but I don't trust him.
Ever since he tried to lay hands on me and I slapped his
ugly face he's had it in for me.'

I didn't like it. It's well known around here that
Danie's on the bottle and the reefers. A man like that
acts wildly. But this particular evening we weren't even
thinking of Danie Jacobs. I'd been listening to the nine
o'clock news on Springbok – and what news! Race
riots in the United States, arguments about the
integration of the black immigrants in Britain, Indians
being slung out of Kenya, Africanization losing white
citizens their jobs in Zambia and Tanzania, and then,
to brighten up the picture, the Russians had launched
a new satellite into deep space. Perhaps one day Earth
will send her first colonists to a new planet, and, if they
do, I hope they'll send a mixed bag that'll interbreed
to create one basic race. I said as much to Veronica and
she laughed.

'You and your grand theories and notions! So now
you want coloured people to inhabit the new planet.
Would you call it Paradise?'

'It would be the home of a mixed race with the
rights and the pride of pioneers. Aristocrats instead of
an anonymous coloured race rejected by all – a race
whose daily bread is frustration and humiliation.'

'Sometimes you talk like the priest.'

'I'm a schoolteacher as my father was before me.'

'There's not much to choose. Preachers and

teachers – wise men, educated, good talkers. Good writers too.'

She nodded towards the radio. 'There's a nice concert on the Afrikaans programme.'

I was tuning it in when we heard the sudden banging on the door. Veronica sat back on her heels, suspicious.

'That's the cheeky way Danie Jacobs knocks, imitating a policeman. What could he be wanting at this hour?'

I went to the door and let him in. It was the hunch-back all right, and my heart jumped into my throat when I saw that a child was with him.

The boy was in a sleeping suit with a warm camel hair dressing-gown and slippers. I had forgotten how beautiful Lex was. Big glowing black eyes, puzzled now, hair crisp and reddish, neat little ears, a wide gay mouth and the pale skin and rosy cheeks that had given Veronica and me the hope that he might be able to belong in a better world than ours. But it was the bright eagerness of his face that made you catch your breath. He was lightly made but strong.

I glanced quickly at Veronica. She was staring at Lex with a mixture of extreme pride and pain in her eyes. Distress was uppermost. If she had risen and touched him she would have cried but she knelt there stunned and afraid for her son. We were still as statues and our silent stillness must have affected the boy, for the

laughing brightness faded from his face and an un-
childish caution took its place. He gazed round him in
dismay, taking everything in – the paper pattern and
the half cut-out dress on the floor, the artificial flowers
in a vase on the table, the picture of Our Lord with the
crook and the black lamb. He looked at that for a long
time, very intently, as if the scene and the picture were
coming back to him. Then his wide perplexed gaze
moved slowly to me and to Veronica with the nervous
awakening of a recognition he could not accept. He
turned to Jacobs who watched him, defiant and
cunning, the whites of his eyes bright red so I knew he
was full of dagga, believing himself to walk tall for an
hour, an instrument of fate. Lex spoke to him, his high
childish voice sharpened by alarm. I know children's
voices. I spot the tremors and the thin lift that gives
them away when they're scared.

'Outside was Fairyland like you said – all lovely
lights – but this isn't the fairy palace you promised
me.'

Jacobs laughed. It was a nasty mocking sound.

'It may not be the fairy palace but you know this
place. Look well!'

Veronica had scrambled to her feet, her scissors
flashing in her hand. She turned to the boy with
hungry aching eyes and then she swung round to face
the hunchback, ashen with shock. If you had cut her
veins and let all the blood out of her body she could

213

hardly have been paler, but her fury was a white hot flame.

'I told you never to bring him here! I told you to let him alone!' She swore at him, her voice shrill and shaking. 'Leave the child here and go! Get out! Voertsek, you dog!'

She was beside herself with rage, and the child began to cry, but Jacobs wasn't scared of her. He took Lex by the shoulders and turned him this way and that. He spoke in thick guttural Afrikaans, which the boy clearly understood.

'Look well at these people, Lex. That man there with the glasses – that coloured teacher and bloody poetry writer. He is your oupa. Yes, look, and you'll remember! And this woman here with the scissors in her hand is your ma. Now come with me and I'll show you her bedroom. In that room you were born and when you were small you slept with her in her bed. This was your home. These are your real folk. This is where you belong.'

The child was terrified. He sobbed and shook his head, he squirmed free of the powerful brown hands that grasped him. His eyes were wide with horror, wet with tears.

'No! No! My grandpa is white, my mother is white. This isn't my home. This is a coloured person's home! I want my mother, I want my own mother! I won't go with you to any other room in this house!'

He had begun to sob hysterically, the tears pouring unchecked down his cheeks, his nose running freely like any neglected coloured child's.

Jacobs grabbed at him, but Lex was quick as lightning, slipping through the thick clumsy fingers and making for the door. Before we could stop him he had opened it and rushed out into the cold night air. We followed but he was through the gate in a flash, dodging a young white man I recognized as Mr Burford who tried to intercept him.

A girl, whose hair was golden under the street lamp, jumped out of a car on the opposite side of the road. She called out 'Lex!' He hesitated and saw her, and cried 'Mommie!' and plunged into the road to go to her.

But the lorry got him first. There was no chance for him. The driver did his best. I shall never forget the screech of brakes and tyres and Veronica's agonized cry as she rushed to the place where he lay. Then she was carrying him here – back to the house he had despised. She laid him gently on the bed in which he had been born in the room he had refused to enter.

Mr Burford and Mrs Symes followed Veronica and her burden into the house. Other people who had collected already pressed around them but we told them to go away. We shut the door on them. An accident brings a crowd from nowhere as honey attracts ants.

Mrs Symes was dazed. She watched Veronica cover the child and fold a clean towel and hold it against the gaping wound in his head.

'Call Dr Pather quickly,' Veronica called to me. But I was already at the telephone getting through to the Indian doctor who lives down our street and who is my friend.

'A white child has been run over by a lorry outside our house. We have him here. Come at once, Dr Pather! He's very badly hurt.'

Outside, people were milling round the lorry which the driver had moved to the side of the road. More surged round our gate. Mr Burford said, 'It'll be necessary to inform the police.'

The hunchback, who stood in the doorway of Veronica's room, echoed the word 'police' as if he liked it.

'Mrs Symes, hold this pad against Lex's head,' said Veronica and Mrs Symes did as she was asked. Her face was stiff and numb with grief as she knelt by the mangled body of the child and staunched the blood that still flowed, staining his copper hair a deeper red.

'Yes, Pa,' said Veronica. 'Ring the police. We all know that number well.'

I went to the phone again while Mr Burford hurried in to be with Mrs Symes and the boy. Dr Pather arrived just then and Veronica met him and showed him into the bedroom. I heard her tell him that Mrs

Symes was Lex's mother and that Mr Burford was a friend. She left them – much as she longed to stay with the child – and joined me in the front room while I telephoned the Police Station.

Jacobs was there in the room where he'd been waiting for us and now he made his fatal mistake. He reached no higher than Veronica's shoulder but he was strong as an ape with his great barrel chest, his long arms and his huge hands. He faced her like an animal looking for a fight.

'I'm going to ask Mr Burford for money,' he said.

She froze.

'When?'

'Now. Before the police come.'

'Why?'

'I shall tell him that if he doesn't pay me I'll give the whole show away. This is my chance!'

'How can you? You kidnapped the child to bring him here. How will that sound to the police?'

'It'll sound all right when I say I was bringing your son to see you because you asked me to.'

'I'll deny that filthy lie!'

'Dr Pather brought Lex into the world. He'll recognize the boy. He'll be my witness.'

Veronica's eyes burned in her deathly face and her right hand felt for her sharp cutting-out scissors on the arm of a chair. She spoke down to him bitterly, her lip drawn back from her teeth, her features distorted with hate and the will to vengeance. I was afraid when I saw her at that moment and heard the sharp intake of her breath. She was no longer my daughter. She was a mad woman. I made as if to go to her and take her arm. But she knocked my hand away and her voice was husky and thin as if her throat was too tense to let words pass. But they did – those terrible words so full of tragic meaning.

'No one – but no one – could recognize the boy as he is now – thanks to you! Have you seen his little face, Danie Jacobs? Have you seen what you did to my lovely boy by bringing him here? I told you not to, I told you I'd kill you if you spoilt his chance!'

She raised her scissors and Jacobs drew back his head as if he feared a blow in the face, but Veronica aimed for the heart. She plunged the scissors deep down into the barrel chest as the hunchback's powerful hands shot up and gripped her neck. I sprang at him then and dragged at his arms and felt his grasp loosen as his knees caved in and he sank on to the floor with a groan, blood oozing from his chest and mouth. The finger-hole handle of the scissors protruded from his breast like the hilt of some strange dagger. He fell with his deformed body spread over the lavender silk and the paper pattern, and the pool of blood grew as the sirens of the police car wailed outside our house. His sightless reddened eyes stared upwards into the light.

'He's dead,' said Veronica hoarsely from her bruised throat. 'The dog is dead.'

Mr Burford stood in the doorway.

'I saw that,' he said. 'And I heard every word. You killed him, Veronica.'

She turned her head and stared at him dumbly.

'But Jacobs had you by the throat. You killed him in self-defence. He was drunk or drugged or both.'

'He'd been smoking dagga and drinking,' I said.

Mr Burford ignored me. He spoke to Veronica slowly and clearly as if he addressed a person too dazed to understand normally.

'Jacobs attacked you, Veronica, and you seized your scissors to defend yourself. I am a lawyer. I will arrange your defence. Don't mention Lex. He has nothing whatsoever to do with this. You don't even know Lex. He's a white child – the child of Mrs Symes. You never saw him before you found him knocked down by the lorry and carried him into your house and called the doctor. You don't know this white child.'

'I don't know the white child,' she repeated with bitter sorrow. 'Danie attacked me and I killed him. It was separate. Nothing to do with Lex.' She understood all right, dazed or not. The bruises were showing violet on the olive skin of her thin neck. She croaked when she spoke.

A police sergeant and a constable came into the

house. I knew the sergeant. He is a big powerful Afrikaner, rough but not a bad fellow. He stood in the doorway of our front room and stared in astonishment at the hunchback.

'What's this, Mr Arendse? You called us about a child run over by a lorry. And here we find Danie Jacobs dead in your house. At all events he looks mighty dead to me.'

Without waiting for an answer he turned to the constable.

'Get on to the surgeon and the photographer right now. The telephone's there in the corner. Now, Mr Arendse?'

I said, 'Sergeant Malan, this is Mr Burford. Perhaps he'd better tell you about the little boy first. I'll explain this afterwards. The child is in the bedroom with his mother, Mrs Symes, and Dr Pather. We got the doctor at once as I told you on the phone.'

Mr Burford acknowledged the introduction.

'I took Mrs Symes and her little boy for a drive to see the lights. It was to be a treat for the child. We came up here off de Waal Drive and parked the car by the schoolhouse. Then the boy and I crossed the road to get a still better view. Mrs Symes stayed in the car. Suddenly and quite unexpectedly the child darted away from me to run back to fetch his mother. He didn't look to right or left, just dashed into the road right in the path of a lorry coming round the bend downhill. The driver couldn't stop in time. He did his best but the accident was inevitable.'

'And then?' asked the sergeant.

Mr Burford cleared his throat.

'And then Miss Arendse ran out of her father's house and saw what had happened. She picked up the injured child and brought him here. Her father telephoned for a doctor. Then the Police Station.'

'And *this* business – did you see what happened to this man?' Sergeant Malan indicated the dead dwarf contemptuously.

'I was with Mrs Symes while the doctor made his examination. On the strength of what he found I came into this room to ask Mr Arendse to let me use the telephone to get through to Port Elizabeth where Mr Symes happens to be on business. I never made that call because it was then that I saw the hunchback with his hands on Miss Arendse's throat and before I could do anything she had stabbed him with her scissors. As you can see, she had been cutting out a dress for a client.'

The sergeant nodded.

'You'd better put through that trunk call to the child's father, Mr Burford.' He switched to English when he spoke to the white man. To us he spoke in Afrikaans and we answered in the same tongue.

He turned to Veronica.

'I'll go in and see the doctor and the child, if you'll

show me the way. After that, Miss Arendse, I shall have to take you into custody. I'm sorry but I have no option. You can make a statement at the station if you wish but you realize it may be used in evidence.'

'I'm a lawyer,' said John Burford. 'I will be glad to act for Miss Arendse *pro deo*.'

'I am grateful,' said my daughter, pale but in control of herself though her faint voice shook painfully. 'This way, Sergeant Malan. And then, if you don't object, I would like to wash my hands.'

She held out her small trembling hands with a gesture of extreme disgust. They were covered with blood and her neat dress too was blood spattered.

'You can clean yourself up,' said the sergeant. 'But you'll need to come with us and you'll appear in the magistrate's court in the morning.'

My stomach turned over. Charged with murder – my daughter! This young woman with her grey face and her bloodied hands was my proud cool Veronica. I was sickened.

'I'll stand bail for her,' said Mr Burford who was at the telephone. 'I saw it happen. The hunchback was one of the crowd who gathered round when the accident occurred. He must have followed Miss Arendse into the house without our noticing. Her father had to shut the door on people crowding after her.'

'You can give your evidence later at the Police Station, Mr Burford. You'll have the opportunity then of talking to Miss Arendse and arranging bail. Now where is the child who was run over?'

'In here.'

Veronica pointed to the closed bedroom door. Sergeant Malan opened it gently and entered the room where Mrs Symes knelt weeping by the bed and Dr Pather stood with his fingers on the fragile wrist of the child.

# 19

# DEREK

---

*'He's in God's hands now'*

I couldn't get a call through to Lindy from Port
Elizabeth on Thursday afternoon because of a freak
hurricane and cloudburst that brought down telephone
wires and grounded all aircraft for several hours.

Our tour had been an unqualified success and our
business meetings had gone off without a hitch so there
was no reason – apart from the weather – why I
shouldn't be able to make the night plane to Cape
Town. My London director, Jim Aston, had no
objections. In fact, he wanted to get away himself.

'If any planes do take off tonight Derek, he said, 'I'd
like to be on my way to Johannesburg. Then I can pick
up tomorrow's connection to London. That'll give me
a clear week-end at home before getting to grips with
Board meetings next week.'

He was elated with the results of our visits to the
major cities. Business was booming, South Africa's
economy was sound and there was plenty of room for
expansion in our business. Of course any idea of my

asking for a transfer would have appeared sheer lunacy and I'd put it right out of my head, but ever since leaving home I'd been on tenterhooks. Now that I knew Danie Jacobs was out to extort money from me or make trouble my peace of mind was in rags. I was feverishly impatient to get back to Lindy and tackle the whole situation one way or another. It simply couldn't be shelved.

I told Jim Aston that, with the telephone dead and the storm at its height, the only thing we could do was to go out to the airport and see for ourselves what the chances were of getting away. He agreed. But before we left the hotel I impressed on the hall porter that if any Cape Town call should come through for me he was to be sure and explain that I hoped to be on my way tonight.

We dined at the airport with our local manager and I did my best to share the general enthusiasm about the future prospects of Aston Brothers. But I kept thinking rather bitterly that if I was going to have to support the hunchback for years to come the suggested raise in my salary would be eaten up as soon as it materialized.

Somewhere around 9.30 we were given the all clear. The southbound Viscount was the first to go and as Jim Aston bade me good-bye he said, 'Be sure and remember me to your pretty Lindy. Next time I come to South Africa I'll bring Eileen and we'll take a holiday at the Cape.'

'That'll be fine,' I said. 'Salaams to Eileen and the family.'

I thanked my Port Elizabeth colleague for his hospitality and launched out into the high wind that buffeted the plane on the runway. I didn't enjoy our take-off and I doubt if the pilot did, so it was a relief when we were fairly steadily airborne above the coastline and the scalloped frills of surf, white and angry on the dark heaving Indian Ocean.

I glanced at my watch. Ten o'clock. I knew Lindy had a dinner date with John Burford but by now she'd be home to give Mark his bottle. Lindy. It had been terrible to leave her with so many real and nebulous fears to haunt her. Lex. His gregarious nature and his mischievous tendency to stray and explore made him particularly vulnerable. I am not usually given to anxiety but that two-hour flight to Cape Town seemed endless. With every moment that passed I became more firmly convinced that Lindy and Lex were in trouble – in desperate need of me perhaps. I told myself that Dr and Mrs van Vuuren could be with their daughter in ten minutes if she wanted them, that John was her willing watchdog, that the hunchback would not act till he had a chance of seeing me and finding out in person to what extent he could bleed me. I tried to stop myself worrying by concentrating on the new developments pending in the South African branches of Aston Brothers.

The steward brought round his trolley of drinks and snacks and I took a whisky and soda. The man in the seat beside mine did the same and began talking about rugby. It would have been churlish to snub him. At last the lights of Cape Town winked up at us, the stewardess made a polite little landing speech in English and Afrikaans, my companion stubbed out his cigarette and we fastened our seat belts.

It was windy and damp with scudding clouds as we filed down the ladder on to the airstrip but there was no rain. I didn't expect anyone to meet me for I was only due to return the following day, so it was an agreeable surprise to find John among those waiting at the barrier. But when I saw his face my heart turned turtle.

'For God's sake what is it?' I asked as we walked to the luggage counter. 'How did you know I was arriving tonight, anyway?'

'I tried to get through to you in P.E. and after an endless delay I got your hotel. They told me you were at the airport hoping to take off for Cape Town. So I phoned air information here and they said one plane was coming through – only one. This one. I took a chance that you'd be on it.'

'What's happened, John? Hold it! That's my suitcase. Let's grab it and go!'

We hurried to his car and I threw my case into the back seat and took my place beside him. He didn't switch the ignition on at once. He sat for a moment with his head in his hands, elbows on the wheel.

'For Christ's sake, John, tell me,' I said. 'Is it Lindy? Is it Lex?'

'Lex.' He looked up, his troubled eyes meeting the questions in mine. 'I'm going to take you to the Red Cross Children's Hospital. He was knocked down by a lorry outside the Arendse house about nine-thirty this evening.'

'Oh, my God! What are his chances?'

He shrugged. 'I don't know, Derek. He's in a coma. Lindy's with him, so is Dr van Vuuren. Her mother's with Mark at your house. Everything possible is being done for poor little Lex.'

On the way to the hospital he told me the whole tale. How Lindy had been dining with him when Minnie had phoned the restaurant, how they'd guessed Jacobs was behind Lex's disappearance and had driven straight to the Arendse house in District Six. It all poured out – the accident, Veronica carrying our injured child into her home, the gentleness of the Indian doctor, Mr Arendse calling the police and Danie Jacobs seizing that moment to threaten Veronica with exposure unless he was paid a first instalment of blackmail money. Veronica raising her scissors and stabbing the hunchback to death.

'Luckily he had his hands on her throat. The bruises

are there. Good evidence. She'll be acquitted on grounds of self-defence. No doubt about that.'

'But Lex – Lex being there at the house . . .'

'Look,' he said, 'we had to take a line about that. We had to make sure the two things – Danie's death and Lex's accident – were in no way connected, as far as the police were concerned. I told them Lindy and I had brought the child up there to see the lights – after all, it is the world's best view of them —'

'It must seem strange to them that you should know that.'

He shrugged impatiently. 'It was the best story I could put up.' He was driving slowly to give us time for discussion before we reached the hospital. 'One has to take a line and stick to it. I explained that I'd parked the car by the schoolhouse and Lex had crossed the road with me to the upper side where the world is really at one's feet, and that – before I could stop him – he'd suddenly darted back to fetch his mother and the lorry driver had been helpless to avert the accident.'

'But Veronica —'

'She and her father ran out of their house when they heard the squeal of the brakes and my cry, and from then on they did what they could to help the white child injured outside their home. A strange child – unknown to them. The business with the hunchback was separate. He followed the crowd that had collected round the house and got in. He was drunk and high on dagga and he assaulted Veronica. She defended herself. That's all. The police swallowed it tonight and they will go on swallowing it.'

Shock had the effect of clearing my brain. The picture John had given me was lucid enough for official consumption, but I saw the personal pitfalls begin to yawn between the truth and the fiction.

'When did you get hold of the van Vuurens?'

'I rang them up when the ambulance called for Lex. Mrs van Vuuren answered the phone. She said she'd go at once to your home and stay with Mark till Lindy came back and her husband would go direct to the hospital and meet Lindy there.'

'By now Minnie will have told my mother-in-law that Lex was kidnapped —'

'No. I saw to that. I rang Minnie straight after I'd spoken to Mrs van Vuuren. Minnie's sick with guilt. She had her radio on so high she didn't hear Lex scrape a chair to the door or pull back the bolt and slip out. She wouldn't have heard either of the kids if they'd cried. As a baby-sitter she was a dead loss. She's ashamed and was only too relieved to be given a story that let her out —'

'What story?'

'That we took Lex with us to see the lights.'

'Thanks,' I said grimly. 'You've had a goddamned busy time. You've thought of everything.'

I've been many sorts of a fool all my life but I've

never been fool enough to underrate my mother-in-law's intelligence, her intuition or her sheer feminine curiosity. All I had to pray for now was that her love for Lindy, her natural generosity and her experience of human nature would help her to forgive and understand the things that can happen to another generation with ideas very different from her own. A moment of truth was on its way and there was nothing we could do about it, no matter what John might hope or contrive.

The great block of the Children's Hospital had come into view opposite Rondebosch Common. My heart sank as John parked near the entrance.

'I'll come in with you,' he said. 'Dr van Vuuren may want you to take Lindy home for a bit. I'll hang around at the reception – and you can let me know the form.'

We made the necessary inquiries from the night porter and I found my way to the surgical ward. There is something very eerie about a hospital at night, the dim lights, the quiet wards where the only sounds are moans and the restlessness of troubled sleep, the nurses moving softly, without the bright smiles of the day, and the knowledge that a visitor in the night means that the fire of life is burning low in someone dearly loved.

'Dr van Vuuren and Mrs Symes are with your little boy,' said the nurse as she left me at the entrance of a small ward. 'Don't worry about disturbing Jannie Nel in the other cot. He's just had an injection to make him sleep.'

My father-in-law's burly figure came round the screens that hid Lex's bed and he made a sign for me to go with him into the corridor. The nurse had disappeared. He took my arm and gave it a brief encouraging squeeze.

'How is he?'

'In a coma. There's been brain injury and it may be a long time – even days – before he regains consciousness. There was a broken leg and arm. He's undergone surgery.'

'Is there any hope for him?'

'Everything possible has been done and will be done, but his condition is critical. He's in God's hands now, my boy.'

In God's hands. He spoke with the simple sincerity that was his hallmark. In spite of all the suffering and sorrow he had witnessed in a life of service he still believed implicitly in the wisdom and compassion of his Creator.

'Derek,' he said. 'I want you to take Lindy home. She's all in and there's nothing she can do here. When – and if – Lex comes round she'll need all her courage and stamina. He'll want her then. Meanwhile she must get some sleep. I'll stay here and if there's the slightest change I'll telephone you at once.'

I nodded, too upset to speak. He led me back into the ward and round the screens. Lindy was sitting by the bed with Lex's limp little hand in hers. There was a cage over his legs, his head was bandaged and dressings covered part of his face, but the soft beautifully curved lips were slightly parted and the long thick lashes lay on his cheeks. His swollen lids were more waxen than I had ever known them in normal sleep.

Lindy raised her head, the short pale hair disordered, her face pinched.

'Darling,' I said. 'My darling . . .'

Dr van Vuuren had left us and I sat beside her on the little stool he must have occupied. I flung my arm about her stooped shoulders.

'Pop wants me to take you home for a few hours' rest. There's nothing we can do here. When he regains consciousness – when he knows people – he'll want you —'

'It could be any time.'

'It could be days, love. And there's Mark to think about. He's only partly weaned, just that night feed to give us more freedom. He needs you too.'

Gently she relinquished the small hand between her own. It lay lifeless on the white cover, the wrist tiny and fragile, the nails livid. She raised her own hands to her breast in a gesture of despair.

'After this . . .' Her eyes were on Lex. 'I don't know. I feel as if everything was drained out of me. Empty.'

Dr van Vuuren had come in. He said gently. 'Go home with Derek, Lindy. I'll be here. At the first sign of Lex waking – or of any change – I'll ring you. You can be here in under ten minutes.'

She kissed the small hand and put the coverlet over it.

'He's so cold,' she said. 'Dear God, make him well.'

She let me lead her away and John drove us home. He didn't come in with us. He said,

'Please let me know any change in Lex's condition as soon as you hear it. I promised Mr Arendse I'd keep in touch with him – any time of the night or day.'

We heard his car rev up and go down the narrow road in the silence of the night. And then there was only the sound of the rising wind and the tossing branches of the oaks.

Mrs van Vuuren opened the door to us. Her eyes were red-rimmed and anxious.

'How is he?'

Lindy shook her head.

'No change,' I said.

'I have coffee waiting for you. Mark's asleep. When I got here Minnie was giving him his bottle. I sent her to bed. She was in such a state that she only made me feel worse.'

She went into the kitchen and returned in a few minutes with a tray of steaming hot coffee and milk.

'When we've had this I'm going home,' she said. 'I'd only be a nuisance here. I have my little car outside.'

'Don't hurry,' said Lindy. 'I won't be able to sleep. I feel as if I'll never sleep again.'

'What happened?' asked Mrs van Vuuren. 'I haven't heard what really happened. Only that there was an accident. Where did John phone from?'

Lindy hesitated. Then she spoke wearily.

'From Veronica Arendse's house. It happened outside her father's house.'

Mrs van Vuuren frowned. 'What was Lex doing there?'

'Seeing the lights . . . seeing Fairyland.'

My mother-in-law has very fine eyes – smoke-blue like Lindy's, but sharper, immensely expressive. They can speak for her, ask questions. They were on her daughter now, pleading.

'Lindy,' she said softly. 'You and I were very close once. After you came back from England we lost it – that closeness. It was as if we spoke to each other through a window – a closed window. Now – tonight – I have to tell you that the day Meisie bit Lex I heard you talk to Veronica in the study. Lex was sleeping on her lap. You told her she must never *never* try to see him again – for his sake, for everybody's sake —'

'You shouldn't have listened.'

'I couldn't help it. You were angry and you let yourself go. You were frightened.'

'Can't this wait till tomorrow?' I cut in. 'Lindy is exhausted.'

'No,' said Lindy, putting down her coffee cup. 'I don't think this can wait. What are you getting at, Mommie?'

'Darling, I drew conclusions that day. Veronica was in England when you adopted Lex. I checked on that. The picture came gradually into focus. Why Lex spoke Afrikaans so quickly and so well, why you were always . . . abrupt with me, as if you feared a conversation. So many small things that go to make up the whole—'

'Please —' I tried to stop her. But again it was Lindy who encouraged her to continue.

'Is it some sort of confession you want from me?'

'No, my child. There is something I want you to know, something that comes from my side of the window. Whatever the story may be – and there *is* a story that accounts for Lex – one that has never been told – I want you two young people to know that I am without criticism. I think it may be a very touching story that proves beyond all else the strength and the worth of Lindy's love for Derek. That is enough for me.'

Lindy uttered a strange little sound that was half a sob. She rose impulsively and went to the chair where her mother sat. She dropped on her knees and buried her face in Mrs van Vuuren's lap. The older woman's hand stroked the fair dishevelled head, and I saw that Lindy was weeping and that it was better so.

I carried the empty coffee cups quietly into the kitchen.

# 20

# LUTHER ARENDSE

---

*'Too much has happened here'*

It was all over – the come and go of ambulance and police van, the removal of the lorry that had struck down my grandson, the questioning at the house and later at the Police Station, and the final nightmare of seeing my daughter led away to the cells on a charge of homicide.

Dr Pather waited for me under the blue light. He drove me back to my home and came in with me.

'A pot of tea, I think,' he said.

So we brewed it in the kitchen and drank it there. I plugged in an electric radiator because the wintry cold – and another more terrible and penetrating chill – seemed to have taken possession of every cell in my body and the marrow of my bones.

It was a house of bloodstains and sorrow in which we sat, silent but for the noisy shout of the wind rattling the windows and hammering on the door. The white and the coloured, the living and the dead had

gone or been taken away, the crowd outside our gate
had dispersed. We were alone.

My friend's dark skin was pitted, his eyes were
shrewd and heavy-lidded, deep wells of the knowledge
of good and evil. The hand that held his tea-cup was
steady and finely made. The Indians have such supple
fingers.

'I've wondered about Lex for three years,' he said.
'Veronica adored that child and it always seemed very
strange to me that she should have parted with him for
adoption. In England. So far away.'

Dr Pather had attended our family for many years.
He had witnessed the death of my wife and the birth of
my grandson. He had not forgotten Lex. Broken and
disfigured by his dreadful injuries, our boy had still
been Lex to Dr Pather. But the doctor must have been
puzzled at finding him in our home with a white
'mother' and Mr Burford. Tonight, at the Station, he
had heard lies and evasions. He had heard us make it
appear that the presence of the boy in our house – the
white child of Mr and Mrs Symes – and the killing of
Jacobs, the hunchback, were totally unrelated. Mr
Burford was wonderfully helpful. He is taking care of
Veronica's defence. He assures me she will be acquitted – that we have nothing to fear on that score. Dr
Pather agrees and his experience of the law courts is
considerable.

'Those bruises on her neck,' he'd said as he drove me

home, 'they are evidence of an assault. She had no weapon other than the scissors with which she had been working earlier in the evening. They were to hand. It was natural that she should have seized them and used them – to save her own life.'

His certainty and Mr Burford's are a great relief to me.

Now, in our tidy kitchen, Dr Pather continued his train of thought about Lex.

'Yes, that adoption story never rang very true to me. I couldn't believe Veronica would give Lex up completely.'

'Veronica loved him enough to give him up,' I said. 'Lex is an exceptional child. You know that.'

'Oh, yes, he was always a leader. He didn't belong here in a slum area. Don't mistake me, Luther. You and I don't actually live in a slum. But it surrounds us and breathes down our necks day and night. Rough, violent people and lay-abouts are on all sides of us here. Lex would have learnt rough violent ways if he had stayed in this neighbourhood.'

'We knew that. We wanted him to have the opportunities of a white person – a far better life than we could give him. The best education, the benefit of a good solid social background. No stigma, no barriers, no doors shut against him on racial grounds, no areas in which he must not live, no beaches where he dare not set foot, no hotels in which he cannot be a guest.'

'You tried to give him to the white world. He could get away with it – for a time.' Dr Pather helped himself to more tea. The Indians are great tea-drinkers. 'Lex is very fair-skinned and he has European features. I suppose Mr Symes – the young white woman's husband – is the father.'

I was too tired for deception. Truth flowed forth in a flood of relief. A good doctor is like a priest. You can say everything – pour out your ills, your sins and your soul – and it remains a closed book.

'You see, Mr Symes is British,' I said. 'He and his wife adopted the child in England. They could never have done it here. In essence, you must realize, our story to our neighbours was true. People found it easy to believe that Veronica had taken her clever light skinned child to England for adoption with a family in a land where there is no racial discrimination. There was no reason for people to guess that the family in question was connected with the Cape.'

'Mrs Symes loves that boy,' said Dr Pather thoughtfully. 'I saw that at once. She must be a fine woman – and tolerant – to accept her husband's son by someone else. Especially in the circumstances. I suppose the hunchback knew the facts? Or guessed them?'

I explained how Jacobs had been night-watchman in the flats where Veronica had worked and Mr Symes had lived, how he had gradually become the go-between. 'That was before he changed – before he became a racketeer and a drug purveyor,' I added.

'So he blackmailed Mr Symes and threatened Veronica with the exposure of the whole story —'

'Which would have ruined Lex's entire future. That was even more important to my daughter than the fact that she and Mr Symes would have been charged with having broken the law. I'm talking too much. Can you make yourself forget what I am telling you?'

'Have no fear. Nobody will ever hear one word of this from me. Nobody will ever know the true identity of the injured child who was brought into this house tonight.'

'I trust you as I would the priest.'

'You can do that. Great sacrifices have been made and great risks were – and are being – taken to give Lex his chance to live white. Is it worth it, Luther Arendse?'

'We thought so at the time. I don't know now. I am a teacher. I recognize an outstanding child when I see one. I wanted Lex to grow up in competition with white children. Perhaps I wanted to see him beat them and reach the top. I was ambitious for him.'

'Yes, in a way I wanted my grandson to vindicate our people and prove what a coloured person could achieve, given a fair chance. I saw that now.'

'You wanted him to be a politician, no doubt. And then, my friend, one day, when he expects to marry – what then? Will he thank you for the great chance that's bound to land him in a greater mess? Let's allow that he goes to the top and gets into Parliament. What when his children are as brown as you or Veronica? Browner perhaps. There's no knowing what those dark genes will produce. They are there for ever – like white prejudice.'

Dr Pather lit a cigarette and the flame of his lighter glowed in the sombre sunken caverns of his deepset eyes.

'For you?' He held out the packet of cheap cigarettes. I took one and accepted a light.

'White prejudice. There's no end to that in our beautiful country,' I said.

'You tell me the hunchback brought Lex here promising to show him Fairyland. Instead he showed the child his own folk. But Lex didn't want you and Veronica. He cried out that his mother and his oupa were white. He wanted Fairyland – not District Six – so he rushed out into the night and was crushed by a lorry. Was it just a lorry that broke up your grandson, Luther? Or was it South Africa's juggernaut – apartheid?'

I was silent. I was seeing again my grandson's large expressive eyes beginning to recall his early childhood as he took in every detail of our front room from the picture of Our Lord with the black sheep to Veronica kneeling on the floor cutting out a pattern as he'd so often seen her do before. Bewilderment had followed the gleam of recognition and then – as Jacobs had forced him to look well at his natural mother – fear had grown in the child's face. Recoil and denial. Veronica and I had roused in him no warmth of remembered affection, but only the growing intuitive terror of some ugly formless truth endangering his whole world. My daughter had stared back at her child, her eyes brimming with heartbreaking hunger. It was all there, her longing to put out her arms and hug Lex to her, but she had not moved, not till that dreadful moment when she sprang up and rushed into the street after him only to carry him back, bleeding and broken, to the room where he'd been born.

Dr Pather looked at his watch.

'It's after midnight, Luther. I have my patients to look after tomorrow and you have your school-children. Don't you think it would be best if you came back to my house tonight? There's a folding bed we could give you. My wife and I have many relatives and there is always somewhere to put a visitor.' He looked round the kitchen of my house of death and spread his fine hands in a helpless gesture of concern. 'This house is not a good place to be alone after all that has happened tonight.'

'Thank you,' I said. 'But I can't come with you. Mr Burford has promised that he will telephone me if Lex . . .' I choked on the word. But he spoke it quietly.

'If Lex dies. My friend, your little boy has suffered

severe brain damage. Sometimes fate is cruel to be kind.' He rose and shrugged himself into his worn overcoat. 'Yes, I understand that you must stay. That call could come tonight.'

I too put on my coat and went to the gate with him. The smell of the rain was on the north-west wind and Dr Pather's long black hair blew wildly round his head as we stood for a moment beside his hard-used car. We looked down at the ships that tossed in the gathering storm and the myriad lights diffused by mist.

'Soon our homes will be taken from us for white habitation,' said Dr Pather. 'You will lose your school up here on the mountainside and I will lose my practice. We folk of District Six will be no more than a cluster of new lights down there on the Flats in Lex's Fairyland.'

'Four generations of my family have lived in this house. My father was head of the school before me,' I said. 'But I won't be sorry to go. Not now. Too much has happened here tonight.'

Dr Pather nodded and got into his car.

I watched him drive away and saw the wheels pass over the sickening new red marks on the grey tarmac. The street lamp showed them up as it had shown up the golden head of the young white woman who had called to Lex as he fled from our home.

Wind-driven clouds raced across the moon and hid the stars, the first spatter of rain beat into my face, cold and pure. The night on Devil's Peak was dark and angry. I turned to go back into my empty house. As I opened the front door the telephone was ringing.

I knew even before I reached it what the news must be. Dr Pather's wisdom and honesty gave me the courage to lift the receiver.